Till Kingdom Come

First published in 2015 by
Istros Books
London, United Kingdom
www.istrosbooks.com

Cover design and typesetting: Davor Pukljak | www.frontispis.hr

ISBN: 978-1-908236-241

Education and Culture DG

Culture Programme

This project has been funded with support from the European Commission. This publication reflects the views only of the author, and the Commission cannot be held responsible for any use which may be made of the information contained therein.

LOTTERY FUNDED

Supported using public funding by
**ARTS COUNCIL
ENGLAND**

ANDREJ NIKOLAIDIS

TILL KINGDOM COME

Translated from the Montenegrin by Will Firth

My gentle mother cannot return.

PAUL CELAN

PROLOGUE: WATER

I think I remember how it all began.

The world was soaking wet like a sponge. By the time February came around, the earth couldn't take another drop.

The winter was unusually mild that year. But it dragged on, as can happen by the Mediterranean, until it swallowed the Spring like an Aesculapian snake eats an egg. The rain poured down day after day, for months. Soon it was half a year. The sardine season was almost over, but people still only went out if they had to, and only in their raincoats. The fishermen gathered every morning in their little cafés by the shore, where everything stinks of fish and seaweed, ready to drink their espresso and head out before dawn as usual. As if the old reality would come back if they held on to their little rituals for long enough. They sat in silence, scrying their coffee sludge, like the last survivors of an exterminated tribe that still doesn't understand why its world has disappeared. They listened in vain to the weather forecast, as bleak as a pagan mass. There was no good news: the rain wouldn't stop, the sea wouldn't drop, and they wouldn't be heading out. The men whose families depended on the catch despaired and drank glass after glass of grappa. In March, only the most persistent went after shad and then vainly stood in the rain trying to sell their fish to non-existent customers. The prawn season, the most profitable of the year, was delayed at first, and then it became clear that it wouldn't take place at all. Even if they had managed to head out, risking their necks in the waves that broke with a roar in the shallow water of the bay, it would have been a pointless effort. The sea was icy cold – just 12 degrees – although May was drawing on. Prawns only come with the warmer currents. They herald the beach tourists, but they wouldn't be coming either, it seemed. The nature that people knew, whose unwritten laws they thought they could rely on, had betrayed them. The things they considered certain failed to occur. What no one in their families had any memory of, and therefore couldn't tell them about, had now happened. The most dogged of the fishermen kept setting their alarm clocks so they could get up at night and tip the water out of their boats, which would fill again even before they made it back to their beds. The others let their vessels sink. When all this finally passed, they would pull them up onto the shore and their skilful hands would clean, repair and re-float them.

Once, out of curiosity, I went down to the marina at three in the morning. I wrapped myself in my raincoat, opened the parasol I had taken from a burglarized storeroom at the beach and sat down on a bench. I opened a bottle of Vat 69 and watched the boats lying at the bottom of the bay for hours. That's what the Ulcinj pirates' fleet must have looked like after it was sunk by the Sultan's navy at the entrance to nearby Valdanos Bay. I thought that same, vacuous thought again and again, vainly trying to think of some other words, until I finished the whisky and threw the empty bottle into the sea. Only then was I able to free myself of the thought of the corsairs' sunken ships. Whoever finds my bottle will get the message: I wanted to say that I have nothing to say. I trudged home, took the basins of rainwater off the bed and slept through until the next evening. It seemed to me, when I finally opened my eyes, that the rain was beating down as if it intended to flatten everything beneath it.

If you wanted to go outside, gumboots were the only suitable foot-wear. But they were no good now either because the water was getting faster and deeper. In the end, wherever you went, you arrived wet up to the waist. The foundations of the houses absorbed the damp, and before the eyes of the tenants it climbed the walls towards the ceiling. Everything we touched was water. We slept on wet sheets under cold, clammy covers. The floorboards were swollen to bursting point. Parquet flooring buckled like the ground after mighty tectonic shifts, such as shook the Earth in pre-human eons. The contours of the floor changed from day to day. Windows, even those with heavy shutters, were no help against the rain. It came with a wild westerly one moment and with a sirocco the next, constantly changed the angle at which it fell, attack-ing now frontally, now from the side, until it had crept through every invisible opening in the walls and woodwork. In their rooms, people made barriers of towels and babies' nappies beneath the windows. When they were sodden, they would be wrung out in the bathroom and quickly returned to the improvised dykes.

Roofs let through water like a poorly controlled national border. Like in a bizarre game of chess, families pulled pots and pans across the floor: Casserole to f3, frying pan to d2. The whole town suffered from sleep deprivation. Everyone finally understood the terrible power of Chinese water torture: the beast dripped all night and drove everyone out of their wits. Some tried to protect themselves from the sound of the drops that fell louder than bombs by stuffing cotton wool in their ears. When even that didn't help, they would turn on their televisions, radios and computers, trying to make noise to block out the monstrous aquatic symphony. Those who had small children would find brief salvation in the children's crying. No one attempted to calm them. They screamed with hunger, fever or colic, but their parents made no attempt to feed them or lull them to sleep. Mothers later recounted guiltily that they had hoped and prayed the crying would go on forever. In the end, the children did tire and fall asleep, and the parents would again be at the mercy of the sound that tormented them. That winter, children learned that crying is useless because no one will help us. And parents learned the lesson that everyone who tries to find salvation in procreation realizes sooner or later: that the children will betray us, just as we betray them.

Ultimately, everyone gave up the struggle. Those who would never have lain in bed and gazed at the ceiling now sat and smoked all night, staring vacantly and watching the containers on the floor fill ever quicker, until they decided it was time to stop emptying them.

The Winter firewood was already used up, and going out to gather new wood in such a gale made no sense. The stove would only smoke, producing no heat, and there were no prospects of it drying the rooms, let alone the walls, where the rising damp was puckering the plaster.

The alleyways ran like rivers. We would long ago have been inundated if the town was not built on a hill. The storm-water drainage became clogged before the New Year. The Central Canal gave way in the middle of April.

Now what we called the Central Canal is an interesting thing: it had not actually been dug for the passage of water. The people of Ulcinj originally made that tunnel because of a different enemy - one of flesh and blood. It led from the old fortress by the shore to half a kilometre inland, all the way to today's promenade, where you find one boutique after another with second-rate Italian wares and jewellers peddling trinkets from Turkey.

At first, the tunnel served for the rapid evacuation of the residents of Kalaja, the fortified Old Town of Ulcinj, who, it should be said, were pirates. They had the custom of plundering Venetian cities, and it seems they particularly liked attacking Perast, a small, wealthy town in the Bay of Kotor, which was practically defenceless because its menfolk were valued mariners in the fleet of *La Serenissima* and thus were constantly *sul viaggio*. Therefore, from time to time the Doge would send the fleet to Ulcinj to take revenge. The Ulcinj pirates evidently considered a good plan of withdrawal no less valuable than a wise plan of attack: the secret tunnel they dug allowed them to flee from the superior Venetian forces. We can just imagine the bewildered Venetian soldiers wandering through the eerily empty Kalaja, where they were met only by starving dogs and seagulls. There was no trace of the corsairs because they had already reached the swamp in the town's hinterland. They made their way through the water lilies and reeds in small, fast rowboats, rushing to *Velika Plaža* beach, where their ships lay hidden. From there, they would embark and launch a counter-attack. With a bit of luck, they would be able to approach the Venetian fleet from behind, while the infidels were still in the fortress, busy with plundering and getting drunk. If the Venetians had already left, never mind: the pirates were still alive, and what had been burnt and stolen they would plunder back again, inshallah. Today we'd say: the main thing is that merchandise changes hands and capital circulates.

People I knew told me that the tunnel was wide enough for a VW Golf to pass through it. I never tested the claim: probably because of the disdain I feel for empirical proof

In any other town, a pirates' escape tunnel would be a tourist attraction. The fact that it was left to become a drain should not be ascribed to a conscious plan of the local authorities, but to their negligence – a unique blend of idleness, impudence and fanaticism – which is interpreted here as consistent non-interference in God's will and His competencies. When Communism collapsed, the local population rediscovered God and started flocking to the mosques, and it became common to complain about dysfunctional municipal services at the local council and for staff to reply that the heap of rubbish that lay stinking in front of your house was there because God wanted it to be:

"If He wanted us to remove the dead horse from your parking slot, we would already have done it," an official told me once.

"If who wanted you to?" I asked nervously.

"Out, get out!" he shouted.

As I hurried away down the corridor, fearing that I had involuntarily experienced proof once again that dialogue is the most overrated thing in the world, I heard the fellow banging the drawers of his desk and repeating to himself: "*If who? Whaddaya mean If who??*"

Searching for a path, the water found the tunnel – it was as simple as that. And then it worked its way out of the tunnel: it breached the fifty-metre tall Cyclopean walls of the Old Town and, true to Kant's definition of the sublime as beauty we experience as fearful, surged into the sea in a mighty torrent.

It may have been a state of emergency, but there was no lack of alcohol in the shops and the black-market cigarette trade still flourished. In Sulyo's crummy shop, where everything was twice as expensive as elsewhere, I was the only buyer anyway. When some local informed me that Sulyo's stocks of Rubin white wine, brandy and *Johnny Walker* were, if not inexhaustible, then at least sufficient for me to drink for another year of floods, all cause for concern disappeared from my mind. I kept buying my cigarettes via the Tadić delivery system: you call them at any hour of the day or night, and the Tadićs bring you a carton of cigarettes within half an hour. The combined IQ of all the Tadićs did not exceed 200, but they had certainly organized a proper little family business: the father sold cigarettes at the market, while his sons darted about town on rattletrap Vespas, delivering them to bars and houses.

"For every four cartons you got a free Coca-Cola," the youngest Tadić told me one evening around midnight as he slugged a litre bottle into my hand.

"Listen," I said to him, "I see you got the idea of the free Cola from pizza delivery services, but if you think about it you"

I realize how absurd it is. Cola may go with pizza, but with cigarettes you need alcohol or coffee."

He looked at me bluntly through the streams of sweat running down his face. He was computing inside.

"We can't give away liquor. That wouldn't pay off," he told me after a pause for computation that seemed as long as the Peloponnesian, Hundred Years', Guatemalan, and all the Punic wars put together.

"Alright, but how about a hundred grams of coffee?"

"Yeah, that would work," he beamed.

"There you go! Do it like that from now on. But I'll keep the Cola all the same – it goes with whisky."

* * *

Now that I was provisioned with everything an honourable man could need, I gladly accepted Maria's invitation to go to Bojana River for the

May-Day holidays. That was typical of her and part of her charm that I found so irresistible: she thought it was perfectly natural and normal to leave a flood-stricken town and go to where there is even more water, just for a change of scene.

She, Goran and Radovan woke me before dawn, bursting into the house like a SWAT unit. Even before I could open my eyes, Maria was rummaging loudly in the kitchen trying to find a vessel to make coffee in, while the other two attacked what was left of last night's Vecchia.

"Come on, get this into you," Radovan passed me a glass of alcohol. "You know what they say: you have to fight fire with fire."

Then Maria arrived with coffee in a Teflon frying pan.

"You don't have any detergent, and this was the only thing that was clean."

Goran found glasses beneath the armchair and the bed, and Maria ladled the coffee into them.

"The three-day rule applies here," he said.

"Which is?" I asked.

"The same as the three-second rule: what's been on the floor for less than three seconds or longer than three days isn't dirty and you can eat and drink out of it," was his reply.

Radovan came from some God-forsaken place in the Krajina borderlands. He claimed he was a close relative of a well-known Bosnian Serb folk-singer. Having a nationalist bard like that in the family opened many doors for him here. That's the kind of time it was. Montenegrin ethno-fascism was comparable with the German variety in terms of its intensity. Its relative lack of coherence and effectiveness at killing can be put down to Montenegrins' legendary laziness and incompetence in organization.

Radovan brought his wife, children and mother with him. His daughters were spectacularly ugly – prime specimens of negative natural selection – but they were not nearly as shocking as his wife. Even the budget of an average Hollywood movie would not have been enough to rectify her appearance. Such disfigurement is a rarity, even in the history of literature. At first she reminded me of one of Tolkien's orcs, but later I realized what ought to have been obvious all along: that God created the woman not in his own likeness, but in that of *Dorian Gray*.

Radovan claimed to be a talented cook and even to have *healing hands*. There was no one who believed it and gave him a job, so he just used his hands for lifting bottles of beer, and he was able to fit more amber fluid in his small body than the laws of physics allowed, I can vouch for that. He was a first-rate liar and intelligent enough to know that you can always rely on people's greed. He found business partners in cafés and bars, where he would booze with them until the small hours. Then, when they were drunk enough, he would ply them with the bizarrest of 'business plans' and ardently describe 'investment opportunities' until they took the bait and turned their pockets inside out for him. The way Radovan conducted his business did not differ substantially from the functionings of global financial capitalism, which is a euphemism for the Ponzi scheme. The *Radovan scheme* differed from the Ponzi scheme only in so far as Radovan never paid a single instalment to anyone – not one cent of profit. Since I was interested in psychoanalysis, I understood that Radovan could be said to be part of real-existing financial capitalism. He never paid any dividends as an enticement for further investment, which would mean greater losses in the long-run, and there was no false hope in making gains – as soon as you gave money to Radovan, you knew you'd get fuck-all back. You could even say that his dealings were closer to The Truth than those of large financial institutions are, and thus closer to Virtue. But there were few who appreciated that, and every now and again he would be beaten up by one of those to whom he had caused grief. But what can you do – everywhere and at all times, people are passionately intolerant of the Truth.

Goran also gave him money several times. Not out of greed, which he had been cured of, but out of a compassion and kindness that probably only still exist in Russian novels. How many times did I tell him, *Don't do it, you know he won't give it back, you know you're throwing your money out the window.* But Goran would just shrug his shoulders, smile and say, *He needs it more than I do.*

Goran was my best and perhaps my only true friend. He lived with his father, a tyrant who first drove Goran's mother out of his kingdom and into her grave, and then pushed his sister into voluntary exile at the age of seventeen. Fleeing head-over-heels from her father, she married the first good-looking, sweet-talking man she met. He would turn out to be the same as her father; but before she realized her mistake, she already had two children, and there was no escape for her any more. Hiding her misery from her husband, she would meet with Goran; she lamented to him, cried and said she'd kill herself then always went back home because she had to feed the children.

Goran worked as a waiter during the day, and at night he went out to sea to try and catch fish to sell so he could put some money his sister's way. Now and then he would rebalance his and his sister's budget by selling the odd matchbox full of grass he'd got from Albania. Goran dealt with the best of intentions, like everything else he did. He spent his free time with me. I couldn't help him – I was never able to help anybody. We drank, told each other intimate things, and then parted, taking all our own misfortunes away with us again. I would watch him from the terrace as he headed away down the path with a light step. He had a proud, dignified bearing that suited him like height suits a cypress.

The morning they came to pick me up, he was particularly cheerful. He put on a brilliant parody of a broad Montenegrin drawl, full of all those lofty and pretentious ways of saying stupid things, which Montenegrins are masters of. He made two or three toasts, each more verbose and vacuous than the one before. Then Maria got up and ordered us to get going.

Radovan's light blue Trabant was waiting for us in the parking slot. He apologized as he tried to unlock the door of the old wreck – his BMW was at the garage.

Even today you can still find discussions on The Web about which was the worst car of all time: the Yugo 45 or the Trabant. But whoever trashes the Trabant has obviously never been in one. Put it this way - if you like to compare a good car with a ship, a Trabant is a rubber dinghy in a force-ten gale. After all, a Trabant can be repaired the same way as people repair boats. The body of the car is made of plastic, and in seaside towns you could see specimens of Trabants among the sails and oars in the maintenance area of the marina, raised up on blocks in a row of yachts and smaller craft. There's just one good thing about the Trabant, and it certainly came out that day in flooded Ulcinj; it doesn't sink.

We set off on the watery voyage to Maria's villa. Maria came from a family of weak fathers and masterly mothers – one where the *men* were married off. It was a mystery as to what had driven her great-grandmother to take her seven-year-old daughter by the hand and leave Trieste, where she had an enormous estate and social standing to match, and end up in Ulcinj, where people gossiped about and feared her. But once here, she bought a property on top of Pinješ Hill, where your gaze goes out across the Adriatic towards Otranto. She had a mansion built there, whose beauty could compare with any *villetta* by Lake Como, and which made everything ever built in Montenegro, including King Nicholas's ostensibly luxurious palace, look like a dump.

That woman would go for afternoon walks by the sea clad in the finest dresses, striding the town and creating a public scandal because the women of Ulcinj rarely went out at that time, and only if accompanied by a man and covered from head to foot.

Maria's grandmother enjoyed a home education: They engaged a governess from Rome, and her piano teacher – only the best would do – came all the way from Moscow.

The self-willed young woman ignored her mother's advice that she stay single, without children. She married a Montenegrin officer from Cetinje, who fled from her when he was sober and beat her when drunk. He died in a Russian prostitute's bed in a quayside brothel by choking on his own vomit while Maria's mother was still in nappies.

Maria's mother, Elletra, followed the family tradition of choosing a wimp for a husband. He did not die young like her father, and immediately after Maria was born Elletra banished him to the outhouse in the pine forest at the far end of the property. Happy there in his pigsty, he tippled and screwed around with the servants. When Elletra could no longer tolerate a bordello in her own backyard, she paid him out and he left for central Serbia to open a café. As Elletra expressly demanded, and in keeping with the contract they both signed, he never tried to contact Maria. Elletra later turned the outhouse into a larder with a collection of alcohol that the best of hotels would be proud of.

And it was to that store that Radovan now ran off, returning with a whole cardboard box of cognac. Elletra's cook came waddling after him. He moved like a penguin because he was lugging two crates of Nikšić beer. Since he was short, the crates scuffed over the asphalt and screeched like Cobain's teeth as he, already poised for suicide, played an *MTV Unplugged* concert on speedball that made him pogo up and down like a wild thing. If I ever come down with delirium tremens... Or rather, *when* I come down with delirium tremens, I won't see white rabbits but a line of penguins with cook's caps on their heads riding down the slopes of Mount Lovćen towards Kotor on empty beer crates and plopping into the sea one after another like ice cubes into whisky, I thought.

"This car is wonderful," Radovan said. "Its only weakness is that the boot is so small."

He zipped back to the larder and this time brought a box of Chardonnay, which he dropped onto Maria's lap, as she had the honour of sitting in the front.

"Just a tick longer, have a smoke and then we'll be off," he said, vanishing into the garden. He came back with a children's inflatable swimming pool, which he made the cook blow up. The fellow sweated from the exertion and I could imagine that he hardly restrained himself from butchering us and stashing the pieces in his freezer. Radovan then roped the swimming pool to the back of the Trabant and put another crate of beer and a few bottles of wine in it, taking care not to overload the vessel and cause it to sink.

As we were leaving, I thought I saw the silhouette of Maria's mother up in the attic window.

A Trabant pulling along a children's swimming pool loaded with alcohol didn't grab the attention of the people of Ulcinj who, as happens with the poor in spirit who live in expectation of famine, cholera and family deaths, had lost all sense of humour and love of the bizarre – the only things of lasting worth among all that has gladdened, frightened or troubled us in our time on this earth.

Ulcinj was deserted and we passed through the town without any great hindrance. The real fun began when we came to the area behind the Velika Plaža beach. From there to Bojana River we had fifteen or so kilometres' drive across the Štoj Plain. In Ulcinj, the water ruled like an autocrat, but in comparison with the reign of terror it unleashed in Štoj it was an enlightened dictatorship, perhaps a bit like the way Tito ruled Yugoslavia. In Štoj, the water was Pol Pot. Bojana River had burst its banks, and Lake Šas had also overflowed. A tide of shit rose from the septic tanks that the residents of Štoj had emptied their bowels into for decades. Dead cows and sheep floated around us. It was hard to avoid them because the water came half way up the windscreen. Our raft of alcohol bumped into bloated carcasses several times, but otherwise Radovan drove a perfect slalom.

"If you were in Noah's situation, what sorts of alcohol would you take with you on the raft?" Maria asked us, holding a perfumed hanky over her nose.

We agreed that it wouldn't be necessary to take a sample of every species of drink because not all of them deserved to exist. The world would be a better place without some drinks, and that is not the end of similarities between alcohol and humankind.

Maria would have liked to turn Noah's raft into a floating wine cellar.

"Guys, for ideological reasons I wouldn't save a single Californian wine," she said. "Some of them are good, some are perhaps even excellent, but Californian wines are anti-wines. Where there is no tradition, there ought not to be any wine either. Do you also get the feeling that they're instant wines concocted like Nescafe? The only thing more scandalous than Californian wines is Californian cognac – because cognac is a perfume among drinks, the essence of tradition."

The rich are fundamentally conservative, and Maria was no exception. However decadent they are, however many transgressions their life is full of, however ardently they promote liberal values, or the manners of their class, and however much compassion they may have for people of colour, the disabled and the LGBT community, the rich want one thing above all: For everything to stay as it is – for them to stay rich, that is.

Goran enthusiastically accepted her thesis. He considered there should only be a place for a very few types of cognac in the new world.

When Radovan announced he would load the raft with good old-fashioned *Rakia*, and add the occasional crate of beer, it became clear that our apocalyptic fantasy was a confirmation of Béla Hamvas's theory that there are wine-, vodka- and beer-drinking peoples.

As far as I'm concerned, there has only ever been one drink – Scotch whisky, single malt. There was no need for any other kinds of alcohol – neither in this world nor in any other. When I later succeeded in life, as they say, and finally had the money for single malt, I didn't drink anything else. A raft loaded with select oak barrels of single malt didn't need to be seen as the seed of a better, future world – it already was the best of all possible worlds.

Entertained by imagining utopias – the path to which is always paved with corpses, or at least carcasses – we arrived at the Bojana River in good spirits. The water had not carried away Goran's hut, although it had been a close call. The small wooden structure, sheathed in tarred and rusty corrugated iron, built to the highest standards of the slums of this world, had proved exceptionally sturdy. There are times when the glass towers fall and all of modernity founders with its information systems and social structures, when gravity overcomes everything that people's pride has put in its way, and then only holes and hovels survive the universal destruction.

The Bojana River wasn't always the cloaca it is today. Fishermen once used to net schools of grey mullet here, and at night they would sit together with local wine and home-grown tobacco telling tales of the good old days and big catches. But the little river had the misfortune of being discovered by rich Muscovites, who brought along their lovers – badly bungled crosses between the male ideal of female beauty and the female need to please the male eye. These Frankenstein-like brides came with their Luis Vuitton handbags and their shrieking Chihuahuas in tow. Later, prostitutes from Novi Pazar opened their all-inclusive spa centres. Then hordes of Montenegrin tycoons descended on the river like tribes of barbarians set on razing Rome to the ground, and this perfect landscape lay in their path, perfectly vulnerable. The moguls' excess of money and lack of taste spawned architectural monsters by the waterside, and in a truly just society they would be publicly executed in the town square and their brains sent to advanced research centres for close examination in the hope that future experts would be able to prevent aesthetic crimes – the most terrible of all.

Radovan sped back to Ulcinj to kill one more wretch's last trace of trust in humanity. The three of us, in a silence disturbed only by the clink of glasses, gazed into the river, which was carrying away the remains of a world lost in the flood. For hours we watched the millions of destructive raindrops compress into the stream of the river. At night, only a few lanterns upstream impaired the perfect darkness we gladly consigned ourselves to.

When Radovan came to collect us three days later, I asked Goran and Maria to wait for me in the car as I prepared to take my leave. I stood on the terrace and let the sorrow flood through my whole being, a sadness that numbed my limbs and then took away my thoughts. I floated in the weightlessness of that potent melancholy, sensing beyond any doubt that something majestic had ended, a grandeur I would remember till my dying day. I knew it was over and that I wouldn't be able to talk about it because, however much detail and eloquence I described it with, the essence would slip away – it was essential to me alone and could not subsequently be interpreted and shared with another person, not even with the future me. I knew that no future intimate bond would be complete enough for that feeling to be shared, because however many words I used, no one would find what I was talking about more significant than some second-hand anecdote.

Our return to Ulcinj ended in catastrophe. Radovan insisted that we drop in for a drink in Štoj on the way. There another guy from the

Krajina borderlands ran a pub called *The Second Chance*. As soon as we set foot in that hole it became clear to us that the name was not without significance – here you had a pretty good chance of picking up AIDS, or syphilis at the very least. Prostitutes roosted in artificial-leather booths lit by imitation candles; the girls were from Moldova, as it turned out. Radovan was a welcome guest here. You could even say a stakeholder. He and his fellow countryman went off for a conspiratorial conversation in 'the office', they told us. The three of us dragged ourselves to the bar. The waitress threw a few bottles of Nikšić beer at us – lukewarm the way bricklayers drink it.

By the time Radovan came back from his 'meeting' and buttoned up his flies, I was starting to slur my words. He insisted we have another drink, claiming he had reason to celebrate. One drink turned into five, or ten, it makes no difference. They carried me out of *The Second Chance* and heaved me into the Trabant.

They woke me when we arrived at a petrol station because our East German wreck finally gave up the ghost. We even tried to jump-start it for a hundred metres or so – in vain, of course. I stumbled several times and fell face down in the slough. Since I was wet and barely able to walk, Maria took me home. I don't know many people who would haul a drunken pig three kilometres through a flooded town in the diluvial rain, fully aware that he would never thank her for it.

Somewhere on the way, I realized from what she told me later, I tried to kiss her. I wasn't pushy, just wet and icky with vomit – my worst possible manifestation. It takes a special feeling for melodrama and tragedy for a man to declare the love he has been harbouring for years to his victim, the unlucky *object* of his love, at the worst possible moment.

She turned me down, though I don't doubt she did it with a lady-like tenderness that would make anyone she turned down love her even more hopelessly. I then gave a romantic speech, whose details she spared me, but clearly it was in keeping with the genre, and thus unbearable. When cynics 'open up their heart', as the phrase goes, they ought to be shot on the spot like rabid dogs. It becomes clear at that moment that the best in the man – his razor-sharp humour, his cold, refined, analytical mind, and the dignified distance he maintains towards everything, including his own life – is actually just a mask. His confession and tears wash away that mask and you have an intellectual wretch before you who has pretended to be an aristocrat of the mind; instead of a rare being whose reason has overcome instinct, you have a rotten hulk kneeling in front of you for whom you feel nothing but disgust.

That's what I told her later, too: "You should have killed me."

"Would you be able to kill me?" she asked with a laugh.

"I'm afraid I don't know any more," I said, but it didn't sound half as good as it would have one day earlier.

She was getting sick of pulling me along against the current, so she called the servants. She took me to a garden, where we sat under an orange tree and waited for the little kitchen hand to come in the pickup. Then they threw me in, drove me home, took off my wet things and left me on the bed, unconscious.

I woke up in Sarajevo, a city I had never been to. I had a clear memory of the previous night. We had been drinking at the *Piccadilly*, a bar behind the cathedral. The father of one of the boys in the group, who owned the place, had the waiter bring us a bottle of whisky as soon as we arrived and got settled in the booths. By ten, we were all drunk – it doesn't take much with teenagers. I wanted to clear my head and decided to go for a walk and get a trolleybus at the Skenderija sports centre. Snow was falling silently through the universe. Each plume of steam from my mouth revealed perfect snowflakes, and whoever saw them would have recognized the structure the world was created from by the principle of endless iteration. I walked past the Markale market hall, the Eternal Flame, and went down Tito Street to the Sarajka department store, where I turned left and stopped outside a bar. I remembered with the precision of the clearest, crispest photograph, although I had never been inside, that I once went in there with a friend the time he bought a matchbox full of hash from the barista before a school excursion to Venice; we smoked it in Cividale del Friuli, another city I had never been to. Recollecting the details of an excursion someone else was on, not me, I arrived at the banks of River Miljacka. It seethed and swirled, flowing as fast as that piddling river could, I recalled.

The trolleybus had broken down at the Olympic Village. I was still drunk and needed to keep walking in the cold air, so I decided not to wait for a bus. I set off for the suburb of Dobrinja, taking a route I had never gone before. The avenue was deserted and I headed down it, ploughing through snow that seemed immaculate. When I unlocked the door of the flat, I heard water flowing in the bathroom. Then I trod on something. I lifted it up from the floor, and in the gleam of light from the upper, glazed section of the bathroom door I saw it was an empty jar of *Zolpidem* sleeping tablets.

I knew the layout of the flat intuitively and without turning on the light, I undressed, went into one of the bedrooms and crashed. I didn't care whose bed it was. I remembered all this when I woke up. I jumped out of bed and went to have a shower because I was supposed to meet a young guy called Amar, whom I didn't know, in the Bazaar that morning. I found a winter coat in the wardrobe and put on my sturdiest boots. I went outside, donned cap and gloves, and was heading for the tram turntable in a Sarajevo suburb when I saw a reflection in a drop of rain on a pine needle, and only then did I realize I was standing on the terrace of my house by the sea; it was night, the 4th May, and the water was draining away from Ulcinj; the sky had opened up, the lights of the town shimmered beneath the stars that had finally come out, and I didn't know what was happening to me.

TIME

1

These spatio-temporal lapses continued in the years that followed and became ever more frequent and prominent. To begin with, they occurred just after I had woken up: Lying in bed in my grandmother's house in Ulcinj, I would open my eyes in Brussels, Paris or London and recall the circumstances that had led me there. I would return five minutes or half an hour later; it was totally unpredictable. Later the lapses became even more common, I'd say almost regular. They could happen at any time: While I was going for a walk, eating a meal or, worst of all, in the middle of a conversation. I would simply fall silent and be somewhere else. The person sitting next to me would call my name, but it didn't work. Most of them simply got up and left. The well-intentioned and devoted ones would call an ambulance. After a few abortive calls, which ended with me coming round in front of the astonished medics and having to apologize, make them a coffee and beg them to be discreet ("My condition is certainly strange, and this is a small town – you know how it is when people find out about things"), the ambulance dispatchers learned to ignore the calls. "Just leave him," they'd say to the good Samaritan. "Get on with your business and don't worry about him. He wanders a bit, and then he comes back as if nothing had happened."

I was unable to perceive any pattern in those lapses or determine what triggered them. At first I thought it might be alcohol. But abstinence didn't help; on the contrary, it made things worse. My condition could be described as an absolute lack of interest in the present, let alone the future. My mind was constantly going into rewind because everything I cared about was in the past.

2

I don't believe those stories about pristine beginnings. True, time spoils everything. And yes, everything gets worse over time. But what is prone to spoil is not necessarily good in the beginning. Everything is bad, even at its inception.

Nor do I believe the stories about the wisdom pronounced by children in their alleged innocence. I'm sure there are children cleverer than I was, and perhaps there have been three-year-olds who walked the earth and had something vital to say. But as a small child I only ever blabbered nonsense. We derive that habit from our childhood, ultimately, and it remains with us even in our so-called mature years and through to our death. There is little consolation when you realize that, until the end, you will write and say things it would have been be wiser not to. And it is small comfort that occasionally people manage to utter a few last words before they die that are not necessarily wise but at least not stupid.

When I was a boy, a year seemed as long as eternity to me. Once my grandmother planted an olive-tree seedling in front of the house. I pranced around the fragile sapling for a while and then decided to be pragmatic and ask when we would be able to pick the first olives.

"In ten years' time," she said. She could just as well have said 'never' – it would have meant the same to me. But from then on I imagined a year like an olive tree. The tree grew as the year passed: quietly and slowly, visible only to the persistent and patient eye.

For me today, the years don't *pass*: They fall like trees – not olive trees but the massive trunks of the northern forests. One minute they're standing tall beneath the sky, the next they're beneath the boots of the lumberjack. Nothing remains of their might except the tremble of the moist earth when those giants come crashing down.

Yes, today the years fall like chainsawed trees. And the warning voice that shouts, 'Timber!' is in vain: they always fall on me. They fall, and it hurts. Maybe the logic is, the more we get battered, the better we can measure time.

Why not throw away our watches and purge all digital devices of the numbers signifying the passage of time? Clocks only ever measure the time of material things: an abstract entity we measure life with, although it is a sterilized and preserved entity that passes life by. *People's time* is entirely different; it doesn't flow uniformly, no two minutes or hours are the same, and its only real measure is the desolation it leaves in its wake.

History is an uninterrupted series of catastrophes – shipwrecks, avalanches, take your pick – where nothing is less important than whether my poor self is going to be dragged under or buried alive. Only arrogant fools expect satisfaction from history; the ordinary, little person is always on the losing end in every brush with history.

And yet that house of ruins, that past built of catastrophes, is all we have.

Maria and I shared a love of Walter Benjamin. Both she and I placed him before all other philosophers, even before the majority of poets, but not above Trakl and Celan. How many bleak winter nights we spent in drunken discussions about his *Arcades* and the *Angel of History*... We both had a passion for knowledge, which is so rare in our time. Living in a provincial backwater surrounded by people who consider selfishness and greed an expression of faultless utilitarianism only intensified that passion. If you've never lived in the backwoods, you don't know to what extent your enjoyment of knowledge sets you apart from others... How complete is the solitude of bibliophiles and thinkers, and how strongly such people bind together and become totally dependent on each other when they meet, against all probability, near the scaffolds of the soul that are our small towns.

I'm sure I still know all of Benjamin's historic-philosophical theses off by heart today, just as Maria did. In the second thesis he says:

"*One of the most remarkable characteristics of human nature*, writes Lotze, *alongside so much selfishness in specific instances, is the freedom from envy, which the present displays toward the future.* Reflection shows us that our image of happiness is thoroughly coloured by the time to which the course of our own existence has assigned us. The kind of happiness that could arouse envy in us exists only in the air we have breathed, among people we could have talked to and women who could have given themselves to us (...)"

3

As if it wasn't bizarre enough that I experienced the memories of other people, whose identity I woke up in, what I considered *my own* memory now lost all narrative continuity over time. Not only did I not know what I had in common with the people I remembered, but I didn't even know what I had in common with the *me* I could remember.

My time seemed to shrink and then to scatter in all directions, forwards and backwards, up and down, into yesterday and tomorrow, exploding into thousands of droplets – fragments I tried again and again to unite, in vain. It was like a ball of wool that rolls down the hill into a stream and ends up all tangled in the waterweed, or like a piece of Czech porcelain from grandmother's chest of drawers that falls to the terracotta floor. It demanded an exceptional effort to re-sort the findings about my own existence and assemble an even slightly convincing narrative about myself. Social contacts were becoming ever harder for me. I was terrified of questions and prop-phrases like 'remember the time we...' or 'you know how...' because I had no answers to them. Actually I did, but they weren't socially acceptable. A short, honest 'no' was out of the question. No, I don't remember. No, I don't know you. No, I really don't know who you are. Lots of little 'noes', which each individually and all together meant one thing: no, I don't know who I am.

In turn, finding consolation in solitude now ceased being a matter of choice and became a necessity. If I wanted to stay outside of institutions I could be put into for my own good by people I knew nothing about, but who claimed to be well-intentioned and even friends, I had to reduce my contacts with the outside world. In that way I created the time I needed to tell myself about myself.

I built myself of water. I tried to give the water shape and hold it back, at least for long enough to glance at myself briefly in the mirror. All that I touched and all that I owned ran between my fingers, trickled away from me, met weirs and then changed course and shape, flowing, falling, gushing away and sinking into the ground, only to well up again, elusive and completely unable to retain any shape.

It was no easy task, but I managed to put my life in order so that I could function in spite of my 'condition', which was constantly worsening. There is only one recipe for happiness, and that is to desire as little as possible. A simple life, even if spent in privation, is the closest you'll get to happiness. When you accept that you have little, most of the problems that have dogged you will vanish – because those problems were fuelled by all the futile efforts to gain more. It's a simple matter: to have a lot takes a lot. Everything I had gained cost me a dearly. It wasn't worth it.

4

I only went out at night, when I could stroll through the deserted town to my heart's content. No one was out in the streets after one in the morning except the schizophrenics hurriedly walking in the squeaky flip-flops they wore summer and winter alike, looking straight ahead. They were my brothers. Their families kept them under lock and key during the day because people in small towns try to hide what is considered shameful. They would let them out at night to get their fill of fresh air and wear themselves out on their sometimes long and always frenzied walks. Before dawn, they would be rounded up, like animals that have strayed from the flock, and returned to their rooms, where they would sleep all day on sedatives.

Drugged-up kids would squeeze into unmanageable cars and race to discos in the suburbs. They didn't notice me. Young couples had fast sex in the woods and on the beaches. They had enough problems of their own even without me turning up – difficulties and embarrassments that, when the night's amorous experiences were recounted the next day, would morph into anatomically impracticable acrobatics and fireworks of passion. Teenage sex is proof that Karl Kraus was right when he maintained that intercourse is a poor substitute for masturbation. Out of consideration for the ordeal they were going through, I always gave the young people a wide berth and tried not to disturb them.

But most of all I liked the dawns. In nature, I have to admit, there is no kitsch. That is also the nicest thing that can be said about nature. It is people's perspective that fouls everything up. When dawn comes like the writing on the wall and the day that arrives in its wake is unwelcome, like all it can possibly bring, there can be no kitsch even in the scene of a person standing at the shore and watching the morning rear up, slowly and terrifying like Godzilla – that gleaming monster one should flee before, to find a refuge and try to survive until the following night. Yes, the dawns were beautiful.

Beauty is difficult.

5

I wrote for the newspapers and that's how I made ends meet. For a while, I used the money my grandmother had left to me, but I soon learned to save, and what I earned from six articles would last until the end of the month.

I wrote quickly and with ease, and what I wrote had an audience. They were commentary pieces at first, fiery and provocative. People liked to read them, especially those who didn't agree with me – and there were quite a lot of them. If you tell people what they don't want to hear in the way they least want to hear it, you'll have their undivided attention and they will become your most loyal readers. I owed every single 'success' of my journalistic career, if we can call it that, to people who would curse and swear when reading my pieces, who would screw up the newspaper and trample on it, only then to wait impatiently for my next article that would drive them around them bend all over again.

Over time, I developed a special style of my own – a kind of hybrid – mixing investigative journalism, cultural criticism and conspiracy theories. The 'investigative' bit shouldn't be taken literally. Naturally I didn't have any 'insider' sources, access to classified information or anything like that. I examined information that had already been published and drafted my articles in the margins. But I dissected these texts like a forensic scientist, and a whole host of things came to light. I discovered logical lapses, discrepancies and incongruities in the statements of the players. If you knew where to look and what to search for, an author's style provided ample information about masked intentions, hush-ups, and the toxic influence of editors and media barons. The lies of politicians melded with the lies of tycoons, who used their media to expose the former's skulduggery. I studied the ownership structures of the media and the ownership structures of firms. I learned to link what I read in the crime columns with the movements of stock-market indices, and I became skilled at recognizing the jargon of party spokespeople in the words of academicians. In my articles, stories about crimes in village schools rubbed shoulders with the theory of the Frankfurt School, the names of bankers stood next to Brecht's, and the tragic fates of Bosnian refugees bore so many similarities to Walter Benjamin's final days. My speculations were no less truthful than supposedly objective information, and were far more interesting.

From the first day on, I felt the deepest disgust for the job I was doing. Journalism is not for the respectable. Which is to say, it should have been the ideal job for me. But there was too much lying and falsity even for my taste.

Today journalists not only play the role of committed thinkers, who communicate important realizations about human existence and work hard to unmask society's hypocrisy. Journalists today are also detectives, exposing what is hidden. It is they who visit criminals in their troubled dreams, where they dread what will be discovered and what dirty work the reporter's X-ray vision will alert the public about, and with the sensitivity about injustice being so great the public prosecutor and police are bound to react. It is a story about bold journalists who uproot society's weeds, a yarn intended for brains readily narcoticized with fairy tales. Journalists are like the animals in the story who band together, holding each other by the tail, and tug and tug until they finally pull a turnip out of the ground.

There is nothing noble in public activism, nothing enlightened or heroic. All that talk about incorruptible public intellectuals and their virtues is a naive fantasy. It's a simple, even trivial matter – a question of the market and the stock exchange, but not of the spirit.

Everyone who participates in 'public life' possesses a certain symbolic capital. The media are just a market for symbolic capital that can be enlarged by the action of the media: Or diminished. Like information, symbolic capital can be transformed into money in one way or another. And just like the dollar, the global currency, symbolic capital has no firm foundation.

The idea of free media flows from the idea of a free market. Both one and the other are pure ideological constructs. Neither one nor the other exists.

The media are a tool for achieving the interests of their owners. Those interests meld with the interests of other ownership structures and political groups, and together they form networks of interest groups.

Publishing in the papers means to serve one of the networks of power. Every communicable truth, however well hidden and dangerous, is a truth to the detriment of one person and the advantage of another, who probably, or rather certainly, has skeletons of their own in the closet. Such a truth is only a partial truth and therefore not the truth at all. Your most brilliant stroke is just the move of a pawn: You are lifted up and put down again on the board so as to keep playing your paltry role as a fighter for the truth, for which you will of course be paid and perhaps even recognized by society.

You'll be the hero of a game in which the media raise the symbolic capital of the interest groups behind them and undermine the symbolic capital of their rivals, who retaliate in kind.

The thought that anyone could consider me the conscience of society was frightening. I despised society, as deeply as can be, and it choosing me to be a guardian of its conscience was irrefutable proof that I was right to do so.

One of my really top-notch pieces, or so I considered it at the time, set off a chain of events that saw me leave the safety of home and reject the precious rituals that had given my existence a degree of predictability and structure. The water flowed out of the narrow, concreted channel it had crept along, never to return.

6

Do you like anniversaries and find them meaningful? Do they give you a sense of security and continuity? People need something to keep them grounded, you think, and just can't allow themselves to be swept along by the floodwaters of time?

Then here's a good anniversary for you.

On Sunday it was four decades since Theodore Robert Bundy, nicknamed Ted, killed Lynda Ann Healy and thus began his killing spree. All that remained of the girl were the blood-stained sheets in her basement flat in Seattle. Two and a half months later Ted killed Donna Gail Manson, who was not related to Charles or Marilyn Manson.

Bundy went on killing, absolutely unhindered, until September of the next year. He was one of the most infamous serial killers. When he was finally arrested, the American authorities were so inept that they allowed him to escape twice: Once only briefly, but the second time, in January 1978, for long enough to break into an isolated house, where he raped two women and beat them to death with a wooden club. One hour later, Ted had moved on and bludgeoned a woman in another house. It was not until July 1979 that he was arrested again and condemned to death.

Ted diligently penned appeal after appeal and, as a God-fearing American, was able to have his execution postponed for ten whole years. He even acted as a police consultant in the case of the Green River serial killer. That slayer was never caught, but Bundy's public-private partnership with the police served as a model for the cooperation of the law-enforcement agencies and the maniac in the film we all love – *The Silence of the Lambs*. Before he was executed, he confessed to twenty murders, although it's estimated that he left over one hundred victims in his path.

Apart from being a serial killer, Ted Bundy was a Republican Party activist.

John Wayne Gacy was... you know, different to Bundy. A Teddy-boy who raped and killed girls – Gacy preferred boys. Bundy was a handsome, charismatic killer, while the namesake of John 'The Duke' Wayne was a paunchy, nondescript boy from the block. Bundy behaved like a star, while Gacy did his best to be friendly to everyone and, if possible, to blend into the background.

Gacy hid the corpses of his victims under his house. When he ran out of space, he threw them in the nearby river. At his trial, he confessed thirty-three murders. He was sentenced to twenty-one life sentences and twelve death penalties.

For the next fourteen years the State was scheduled to administer him the lethal injection, Gacy claimed he himself was 'the thirty-fourth victim', in other words that he was the victim of a conspiracy to frame him.

Apart from being a serial killer, J.W. Gacy was a Democratic Party activist.

With a little luck and more caution, both men could have gone undetected. Two so cunning and capable guys could have achieved a lot if only they had concentrated on politics – if they had killed legally.

In a world just a bit more twisted and just a little further to the right, Ted Bundy and John Wayne Gacy could both have become American presidential candidates. This hypothesis is not as far-fetched as it might sound.

A serial killer is a perfect candidate for the presidency of any large country. He is already prepared for what awaits him: the sowing of death. Whoever becomes President of the USA – or Russia or France or Prime Minister of Britain, it makes no difference – goes on to become a killer. It is not usual, as far as we know, for American presidents to cruise their country massacring young women and men before taking their oath of office. And yet, under their command, the armed forces and secret services will kill countless people throughout the world.

Bundy and Gacy mistreated their captives, just as the presidents' soldiers would do in Iraq, Guantanamo and CIA concentration camps in Europe. How many Bundys and Gacys are wearing American uniforms today? How many prisons are there where these maniacs torture their victims in the name of the Constitution and the American people?

A US president must also have a wife, of course.

Americans are fascinated by serial killers and presidents, and as he was waiting on death row, Ted Bundy received love letters every day from beautiful women, many of whom looked just like his victims – brunettes with long hair parted in the middle. Before he was executed, he chose one of them to be his bride and managed to ensure offspring. Thanks to artificial insemination, the lady bore Ted Bundy's child. It would have been a shame if those genes had been lost.

Gacy had an even more dynamic prison life, full of fine art and the proceeds from it. And despite being behind bars, he maintained a romantic involvement with a twice-divorced mother of eight. She used Gacy as a marketing tool and managed to get on several talk shows. 'John Wayne' himself took to painting in a big way. He produced self-portraits and pictures of clowns – before his time in jail he used to dress up as a clown at children's parties.

His social streak, after all, was why his neighbours couldn't believe someone as altruistic as Gacy was actually a killer. His paintings fetched prices of up to several hundred thousand dollars, and when the artist died he left behind a substantial endowment. The State was furious at him having acquired wealth through being a serial killer and sued Gacy's estate to recoup the costs of his fourteen years in prison.

The State was so furious because it jealously guards its exclusive right to kill with impunity: And even makes a profit from it. So if the State is a repressive, murderous machine, why couldn't it also be run by a killer – one who knows what the business is about?

I find that the whole debate about the abolition of the death penalty misses the mark. The nature of the State is not going to change if the State decides to stop frying murderers on the electric chair. Abolishing the death penalty does not do away with the State's right to kill, as is often misleadingly claimed, because the State will still have the right to wage war and to run secret services with all they death they sow. The State will kill for as long as it exists. And it will kill more, the bigger and more powerful it is.

But what a terrible, crying shame it was that we never saw a presidential debate between Ted Bundy and Wayne Gacy: their heated exchange on foreign policy or the issue of bringing American troops home from abroad; and both candidates swearing, although they were serial killers, that the life of American citizens was sacred to them. Gacy would probably have flirted with the gay community and had the sympathies of liberal commentators. Ted Bundy, as a Republican, would probably have opposed abortion from a 'pro-life' position.

A perfect crime is not one where all traces are removed, thus making it a mystery even for the cleverest investigator. A true perfect crime is one that is not even recognized as a crime, one that is legalised and becomes an integral part of society, tradition, civilization and politics – such a crime, ultimately, serves as the basis of every State.

7

Ten days after the article was published, the phone rang. A warbly female voice announced she was calling from the Ministry of the Interior and advised me that I had the honour of receiving a call from the minister himself: *The boss wants to speak to you.*

Minister Mandušić was most cordial. If anyone had listened to a recording of our conversation, they would have concluded we were old acquaintances who had gone through a lot together: Sacksful of shared memories and, even more importantly, shared secrets. I assumed that Mandušić knew a lot about me – this may be a failed state, but the secret services in such states work with particular effectiveness. I also knew a thing or two about him, in a way. The assumption that one knew things about the other was his reason for inviting me to meet him, and it was mine for accepting the invitation.

Goran drove me to Podgorica. We took the long way, via the Petrovačka Gora mountain range, because it was a rainy day and Goran thought we had a good chance of meeting the 'Lady in White'.

The Lady, people told me, was a spirit that had the habit of waylaying superstitious travellers in the deep of the night, especially when mist and rain turned the winding road into a Gothic *mise-en-scène*. She didn't steal souls or make travellers pay a black toll: All she took was a tribute in fear. And fear is cheap and never runs out.

Goran knew several people who claimed to have seen the Lady. They said she came flying up to the car, clung to the bonnet and pressed her bloody, pockmarked face against the windscreen. However fast they drove and however much they jolted around the curves, they were never able to shake her off the car. When she went, it was because she wanted to. She left behind a trail of blood and pus on the bonnet, which stank for months afterwards and was impossible to clean off.

"Alright then," I said to my friend, who, when he wasn't drinking with me, spent his free time watching horror films, being the owner of the largest collection of ghost, Gothic and zombie movies in Eastern Europe. "What would you do if we met the Lady?"

"I'd say: Hey sis, where ya been all this time?", he shouted. He added that, for him, there was no difference between his Lady and the 'Lady of Medugorje'. In searching for the 'Lady in White', he hoped for the same thing that takes fervent Catholics on pilgrimages to Međugorje in Herzegovina: a miracle to confirm his faith. Of course, even if he doesn't meet her, he believes – no, he *knows* – that vampires exist and that everyone who does not obstinately close his eyes to the idea of spirits can see them.

Passing through the wilds of the Petrovačka Gora range, we were caught unawares not by the Lady but by a police patrol. A dumpy policeman literally came rolling out of the forest and levelled his stop sign at us like Father Karras waved the cross above the body of possessed young Regan.

"How ya goin', boys?" he drawled, leaning in the car window. That was overly familiar for my taste. I replied coldly and officially, the way he ought to have addressed us. People like that take it as an insult if you don't go along with their chumminess. Nothing irritates them more than elementary decency, and it makes their hair stand on end like a wildcat's. Montenegro is full of characters like that. Here dirty old men you see for the first time in your life ask you, 'So what are you fucking, boys?' and reach for their shrivelled groin with gusto. And it's not a rhetorical question: they really do expect you to stop in the middle of the street or on the terrace of a café – wherever you've had the misfortune of running into them – and whatever you've just been doing or intend to do afterwards, they insist that you scrap your plans and describe your last act of coitus for them in detail.

The policeman made no bones about being offended. If I had spat in his face it would have caused less affront than me being aloof.

"Alright, sir. Now, boys –," he said and chuckled at his own joke, which eluded me, "drive slowly, the boss is expecting you. Come on now, skedaddle," he added and patted Goran's car like he might the flanks of a horse.

"And they say there's no functioning State here!" Goran sighed and put his foot to the floor.

Later, when I thought back to that day, I'd understand that it was then that I first noticed a sign of 'The Hand'. As these things go, the terrible realization did not hit me until afterwards, when it was too late: what if there's a hand guiding me through life? Not a good hand from above, nothing like that. It was more likely a black hand from below; from the police and intelligence-service underground. Nothing metaphysical or transcendental; no kind of god. But nevertheless, very much real and existing. The hand of some monstrous thing that only just comes into view, too big for me ever to see the whole of it, and large enough to block my view of everything else. In the years that followed, I would come to doubt that anything I did was of my own free will. I would see the volition of that 'Black Hand' in my actions and would convince myself of its existence innumerable times. Yes, it was omnipresent, particularly when it seemed there was no one except me. Back then in Goran's car up in the Petrovačka Gora range, I would doubt that my article was the real reason for the Minister's call. *What if he knows a lot more about me than I thought? What if I don't know anything about him, especially not what I thought I knew?* I asked myself.

We were in the grips of paranoia when we arrived in Podgorica. Goran was also troubled: what if that policeman had searched us and found the grass? What if the fatso had just been on patrol and a proper police ambush was waiting for us on the road into the city? My friend had decided to combine the pleasant with the useful, as they say, and had brought along a few little packets of Albanian ganja. There were buyers in Podgorica. I was convinced that the police weren't interested in small-time dealers, when not even the big ones interested them. But dark thoughts about what the minister could want of me whirled like a swarm of flies, whose persistent buzzing left me thinking just one thing: *This is not going to end well.*

We arrived at the Ministry of the Interior. A bay was reserved for us in the parking lot at the front. An officer pointed us the way and gave a conspiratorial nod. As we were entering the building, Goran remembered that he still had the grass on him. He admitted this to me in a whisper as we were waiting for security to search us.

"Perhaps this is the right moment to run out to the car," I suggested.

"I forgot to lock the car, d'oh!" he groaned theatrically and smacked his forehead.

"Don't worry, it's in safe hands," a seven-foot man said, who now introduced himself as Head of Security. "There's no need for a search, they're with me," he added for the police at the entrance.

The wall of men in blue opened wide before us like the gates of hell.

We went up the broad, marble stairs to the first floor, where the Minister's office was.

"I'm leaving you now. You're in good hands," the hulk said.

The door of the office opened. Red carpet, mahogany-panelled walls, photographs of the Minister's meetings with foreign statesmen, glass cases of gifts he had been given at those meetings, among them a 1886 Winchester rifle from the director of the CIA. Then the secretary, whose birdlike voice I recognized. She ushered me in to see the minister. Goran waited in the front room, where the secretary promised to bring him coffee and a cold drink.

The office was filled with massive leather furniture while on the floor lay a three-finger thick Persian rug, as soft as cotton wool, capable of defying gravity, which I couldn't restrain myself from taking a few steps on, as light as a moonwalk. A Montenegrin flag on a pole in the corner. More mahogany, more showcases with gifts. A small library: The collected works of Marx and Lenin, several editions of the *Letters of Petar I Petrović-Njegoš*, the Montenegrin prince-bishop, a handful of titles on Russian-Montenegrin friendship, Catherine Albanese's *America: Religions and Religion*, a whole shelf of conspiracy-theory books on Freemasons and Illuminati. A desk, a real masterpiece of the furniture of power, dominated the room. It plainly divided the world into the space in front of it and that behind it.

I cleared my throat discreetly a few times to try and announce my presence. There was no answer. I looked around the room searching for cameras. I thought I saw one above the bookshelves, but it was just a smoke detector.

Then I heard a toilet flush and the Minister, smelling of soap, emerged from a tract hidden behind the bookshelves.

"Ah, there you are," he said in mock surprise. "You caught me at an awkward moment. What can I say –," eloquent Mandušić continued, "the powerful have to shit too. We are also organic, very much so. Do you know the greatest desire of everyone in power is to escape the terror of nature and to overcome their biological limitations. That's why those in power hide away in monumental buildings, in temples of marble and steel. That's why they love monuments, because they don't decay. And that's why the photograph is their favourite format, because it freezes time and turns it to stone. If we could command it, time would stop right here in the moment of our greatest triumph and our calm, firm rule. But to rule also means to await the moment when the mob will lynch us. That's not on the photo; it doesn't show the next episode with its arrests, public humiliation and perhaps even public execution. There's just the suspended light and suspended time of the moment before the fall."

He threw his left arm over my shoulder. "Come on, let's go into my study."

He led me into a small room with piles of books and files on the floor. As I reclined in the armchair, I surveyed the titles: Melville, Auden, Dostoyevsky, Pound, Hegel, and Benjamin...

"You know I have a PhD in literature from Zagreb," he said. "A lot of people wonder why I've ended up here, heading the police force. It's quite simple, actually: Imagine the State as an enormous novel, a text that is continuously evolving and being written. My job, like that of a writer, is to have complete control over all the characters in the story. Who will understand them, with all their desires, hopes and ambitions, if not me? Who else can say what a character will do on the next page if not the writer, if not me? In society, as in a good novel, nothing happens spontaneously. Everything flows from the logic of the story and the nature of the characters. The ideal police officer doesn't solve crimes that have already happened but prevents future ones. It's not about interpreting the text but writing it."

He took a bottle out of the cabinet – Aberlour single malt, twelve years old.

"Your favourite, if I'm not mistaken," he winked. 'What can you do? People bring bottles. You know what we Montenegrins are like. It's a nice custom, if you ask me. Ultimately it's civilized, if we recall that they once used to bring dead animals, or even worse, children... Note the element of progress: It's better for them to offer a bottle of whisky than an ox's heart, isn't it? But now we're a candidate for joining the European Union, this custom like so many others, will die out. Because it's corruption, you think? I'm rather an expert on corruption, believe you me, and this is not corruption,' he declared, raising his glass of whisky.

"You see, that's exactly why I've called you. Not because of corruption –," he said through a laugh, "but to do with the European Union."

"The accession process 'is under way', as they say, and I have to travel to conferences on security in Europe. Speeches are held, as you can imagine. We shepherds come together and talk to each other about the importance of properly supervising the flock."

"Now... I'm a proud man; that should come as no surprise. I'm not prepared to read out claptrap at those meetings. I have a horde of advisors, but I use them for just one thing: I ask them for their opinion, and then I do exactly the opposite of what they advise. Unfortunately I don't have time to devote to those speeches. So now we finally come to you, and I apologize for keeping you in suspense. I've been following your pieces for a long time. In fact, you could say I'm a devoted reader of yours. You remind me of myself when I was younger. Your delusions are charming and you argue them elegantly, with extraordinary zeal and conviction. That's what attracted me to your pieces. Don't get me wrong: I know very well you're not right, but still you almost convince me of your positions. That's a rare talent, and I could make good use of it. So I'm making you an offer. You can give up writing for the papers. Nothing really important is written about in the papers, nor are any problems resolved in newsprint. I'd like you to write for me. Be my ghost-writer. There's no occupation like that within the system, of course, so you won't have to come in to work: your workplace will be your own study. If you want to move to Podgorica, we'll rent a flat for you. If not, we can deal with everything over the phone. There are no secrets here – everything is wiretapped anyway, including this conversation. The pay isn't great, and government employees aren't rich, as you know, but it's certainly more than you earn now. That's it, that's all. There are no hidden conditions and no contract you have to sign in blood. It's a clean, strictly business relationship. What do you think?" he asked as he poured me another whisky.

"I need to think it over."

"Just what I expected you to say," he replied. "I wouldn't employ a gutless yes-man."

He saw me to the door, and before we parted he added:

"You know, after every meeting, however important it was, I don't think about what else I could have said. My only thought is what would best have been left *unsaid*. Remember that when you write for me."

Goran later told me I came out of the Minister's office *a different man* – that's how he put it.

I was silent all the way home, as if I was thinking about something important. Actually I had fallen into a torpor, equally distant from all thought and all emotion, a state where I felt exceptionally at ease, so much so that I wanted it to last forever. I waited in the car until Goran had sold his weed, and then we travelled on home without a word. I invited him in for a drink, but he had promised to take his sister to the shops. He would see me that night, he said.

I went into my room and studied it; the rickety double bed with its stained blankets that cried out for a dry-cleaning; the threadbare plush armchair; the wooden desk; the ashtray full of cigarette butts; the glasses with the remains of the previous night's drink; the pictures on the spotty walls. Everything was in its place. Everything was the same.

But nothing was the same any more.

8

The newspapers reported on my appointment for weeks. Column-ists wrote reams about the relationship between intellectuals and the system and about me betraying the principles of free journalism. NGO activists issued lengthy statements expressing abhorrence at the idea of a journalist working for the police. And one writer, wanting to explain the dimension of my fall, told an anecdote about Goethe and Bee-thoven. The two of them were walking along a forest track, he wrote, and a duke's coach was coming from the other direction. Goethe, if I remember correctly (or was it Beethoven?) stepped aside to avoid the horses that were bearing down on them with frightening speed. Beethoven (or was it Goethe?) refused to get out of the way. When the coach had passed, Beethoven (or perhaps it was Goethe after all?) blamed his friend for stepping aside to let the nobleman and his horses pass. The world is full of bigwigs, Goethe said, or was it Beethoven; one of them was definitely Goethe – or was one of them definitely Bee-thoven? I sent that idiot an email to thank him. I'm not sure if you consider me Goethe, or perhaps Beethoven, I wrote, but either way I'm eternally grateful: no one has ever made me a nicer compliment.

If I was able to see myself as a victim, if only for a moment, I would have called the whole thing a media lynch. But I refuse to be a victim, and there's nothing I dislike more than people who complain all day about their rights being threatened. That's why it's hard for me to live in this world, where everyone seems to just want to be a victim.

Since that's the way things are, I viewed the media's sudden concern for my humble self with utter contempt. It felt like a bucket of slops had been tipped over me by the two tycoons whose newspapers I wrote for before accepting Mandušić's offer. Whether they had nothing better to do or it was ordinary human malice, those two criminals acted as if they were offended by me no longer wanting to work for the pittance they paid. Minister Mandušić gave me more than just moral support – he furnished me with a list of people in the 'public eye' who were overtly or covertly in the pay of the two-mentioned crooks. Interestingly, the names on the list coincided with names of the people who had dis-paraged me in the papers, and more importantly still, with the names on a list of public figures that were also on the payroll of Mandušić's secret police. Public intellectuals were secret agents and vice versa: Free journalists were spies, and vice versa. Independent media were really secret-police bulletins, and papers were edited by police officers, while newspaper editors did police work. Who on earth could make head or tail of this? I was ultimately glad about my decision to no longer participate in public life, which was nothing but the meanest brothel, where people careless enough to open the papers or turn on the television picked up deadly viruses and nasty contagions and carried them back to their homes.

If you have the misfortune to be written about in the papers, people descend on you like flies are drawn to shit. One day your name is mentioned in the press or on the TV news, and the next you won't be able to walk down the street for all the creeps who want to speak to you. Whether they criticize you or offer what they think is well-meaning advice, it leaves you feeling equally polluted and smelly. There is nothing that can remove that horrid, stinking aura from you except anonymity. And that is hard to regain, especially in a small country like Montenegro, where unfortunately people have good memories, are idle, and above all prone to malice. If you once become famous, or if you disgrace yourself, it doesn't matter which, you have to carry that stigma for the rest of your life.

But when that big, black blowfly came thumping on my door one morning at the crack of dawn, before the dustmen had even collected the rubbish, and introduced itself as *Great-uncle Tripko, your grandmother's brother – don't you remember me?* Things had really gone too far.

9

The night before, Goran, Maria and I had knocked off two bottles of Cardhu that Mandušić had sent me. The whisky ran out before midnight and unfortunately I didn't have anything else in the house except beer. The shops were closed at that hour in winter, so I had no choice but to call my neighbour Ramiz to help. He was someone you could rely on in an emergency. And we didn't need to wait a thousand years for our saviour. Before five minutes had passed, Ramiz burst into the house with a box full of Rubin brandy.

"Let me give you young 'uns a word of advice –," he said with a slur, "whisky is good but always in short supply."

Ramiz received a small Swedish pension or regular social-security payment, I never found out exactly what. He claimed to have 'earned' these means for a comfortable retirement simply by being in Stockholm. When he saw an open manhole, he seized the opportunity and jumped in, and later he sued the Government. He wore a leather waistcoat all year round with two letters emblazoned on it: MR. That stood for Master of Rubin. He proudly bore that self-awarded title, and that was how he lived – and died, after having sent truckloads of Rubin brandy through his liver.

Anyway, where was I... *Great-uncle Tripko, my grandmother's brother*, woke me from my drunken slumber. I had never seen the fellow in my life, and that's how things should have stayed. He burst into the house, demanded coffee, and while a huge pneumatic hammer was pounding in my head, he began a monologue about why he had lugged his old arse all the way from Višegrad, Bosnia.

He blathered away for a good half hour, but it was clear from the first sentence, no, from the first word, no, from the first grim smile illuminated by a golden tooth (in place of the second left upper incisor, if I'm not mistaken), that Tripko wanted money.

Gruesome war crimes were committed in Višegrad. Anyone who's interested, although that's not many, can learn more or less everything about those crimes today. But one thing is never mentioned when people talk about the war crimes, and I can't help but put it down to hypocrisy. The terrible thing to do with the war crimes is not just that some people were killed, but that some others weren't – Uncle Tripko for example, I thought that morning.

I bet he watched and applauded while Muslims were being butchered on the bridge over the River Drina, if he wasn't assisting the killers already. No doubt about it: That's the sort of mug he was. One look at Tripko and you could reconstruct his entire life with all the details of that worthless existence: a junior officer in the Yugoslav People's Army, who took early retirement and was now as fit as a fiddle at the age of seventy because he never had to work hard, his wife bore the load of the labour for him, and he beat her and cheated on her with waitresses and cashiers until she died of a heart attack. This beast had now read in the paper that a relation of his, 'a bosom relative' as he put it, had landed himself an important position, so now he came rocking up to get his share of the booty. "Who can help each other if not family?" he philosophized as he slurped his coffee.

"Listen," I finally said to him, "I'm not sure we know each other, but that doesn't change a thing. Money is not an issue – there is no money. Even if I had any I wouldn't give it to you. If it makes things easier for you, take a look around. Do you see the hole I live in? Do you think some moneybags lives here?"

Then my uncle reared up and transfixed me with a gaze of primordial hatred.

"You little shit," he thundered, "do you think you can get rid of me like you shake a tick off your trouser leg? No money, eh? a cushy position but no dough? Do you think Tripko's an old duffer? You don't know Tripko, sonny. Uncle Tripko will teach you to mess him around! This house you live in, this *hole*, as you call it – is mine. You think it was left to you by your grandmother, do you? But your grandmother wasn't your grandmother. My kind sister, bless her soul, brought you up like her own son because she had a heart as big as Russia, though you weren't kith or kin. But I won't have you loafing around here by the sea in my house while I rot away in a thirty-square metre hovel by the Drina. I go to sleep at night not knowing if I'll be kidnapped and wake up downstream! And to see you here like this!"

As strong as a bear, he grabbed me by the throat and pinned me against the wall: "This is *my* house, *you're* the stranger here, and you dare to fuck me around!" he hissed. "You think you're a clever Dick, don't you. You think you're better than me – you, a whore's little bastard, the son of that monster!"

Thus spoke Tripko, and he was a man of the old school: He honestly believed that every argumentation, however logical and rhetorically powerful, became even deadlier when backed up by a degree of brute physical force. Finally he threw me onto the bed like a stuffed toy and stormed out of the house like a huge, retarded boy in a huff, slamming the door behind him.

"You'll be hearing from me. Start packing and get out of my house quick smart!" he shouted from the terrace.

I lay on the bed and closed my eyes. All I could think of in the moment before sleep took me was what an utter scourge he was.

10

I never saw Uncle Tripko again. His solicitor didn't call me, and no letter with a court summons or eviction notice ever came.

Nor did Tripko ever arrive home in Višegrad.

It seems his neighbours alerted the police two weeks after he left for Montenegro, where, he told them in confidence, he had some important real-estate business to attend to. The papers reported that his car was found near Lake Piva, in front of a tunnel on the road from Plužine to the Bosnian border. Although divers were unable to locate his body, the investigation established that Tripko committed suicide by jumping into the lake. No farewell letter was found. The details of his visit to Montenegro were not known, the police announced.

Tripko disappeared, and with him the danger of me losing the house. What a lovely and apt happy ending, I thought at first. Alas, there is only one happy ending – the Apocalypse – even if it is only a promise. Everything else is just an open ending, a continuous series of open endings, whose resolution not only resolves nothing but further complicates already unbearably complicated things. Whenever someone says to me, 'That's simple', I think: Sure, mate, everything's simple if you've got no idea. To an ignoramus, everything seems self-explanatory, and 'obviously' is their favourite word.

In fact, everything that exists is complicated beyond our power of comprehension. If you think twice about things, if you re-examine your own assumptions and convictions, everything you think you know will turn out to be as enormous and mysterious as the Sphinx.

I tried my very hardest, but I couldn't forget Tripko's words. The fire belched by that ireful prophet-of-doom swept away the serenity of my world. All that remained of my peace and calm was the cold smoke rising from the scorched landscape I had lulled my existence into.

What the hell did he mean about me not being my grandmother's grandson? Was that undeniably vile man really such a rotter as to openly hate his sister's daughter? What could my unfortunate mother, whom my grandmother always spoke of as a saint and martyr, have done to offend him? Why did the papers write about the disappearance of Tripko Pavlović – not Hafner, but Pavlović? The man in the photos, which accompanied the articles, was Uncle Tripko. Right man - , wrong surname.

Why did my grandmother never mention that she had a brother? Why the mix-up with surnames of close relatives? What else did that good woman keep secret from me?

11

After Tripko left *my* house and vanished into the void, I slept the whole day and the next night. I woke up beside my grandmother's grave. There were two very well-paid, lazy gravediggers, whom I felt were taking absolutely ages to do the job. I hadn't informed anyone about grandmother's death. I remember I didn't have an obituary notice printed, and of course I didn't permit the outrageous perversion of announcing her death in the newspaper. Although the cemetery was unfamiliar, I knew I was in Bar. I didn't know anyone in that city and had her buried there so I could be sure nobody would come along and spoil things – those were my thoughts as I prepared the details of the funeral, I knew.

I had paid the workers well. They misunderstood the gesture and considered it their duty to pretend to be deeply touched by her death. When we'd buried her I couldn't make them leave the grave. They just stood there, crossing themselves ceaselessly in compensation for the lack of mourners. "The poor woman; to die so alone and for no one to come to the burial," one lamented. "May the dark earth rest lightly on her after such martyrdom," the other said. I desperately wanted to be alone but they refused to go. Instead, they came up with new and ever more pathetic folkloric creations. This introduced an element of the ridiculous, which was superfluous because funerals are ridiculous as they are, in common with all situations where people feel obliged to be serious and dignified. I was reminded once again that the nicest thing we can say about a person is that one day they will die and cease to bother us. In the end, I had to pay the workers double before they finally agreed to leave. At a cemetery, surrounded by the dead, we're at the source of cognizance. At a cemetery we learn at first glance all we need to know about life - that we're going to die. I sat down on the dry-stone-wall by my grandmother's grave and lit a cigarette.

The wind blew several snowflakes into my face. I looked around and saw that I was alone in the cemetery, which extended out to all four corners of the world. Row upon row of stone crosses marched to the horizon, where threatening black clouds were mustering. War is the father of all things, I remember thinking: An army of dead against a heavenly army. Thunder rumbled through the valley.

Both the cemetery and I witnessed those sound effects of nature in impassive silence. Wherever I looked, I saw graves mounted with crosses, upright and dignified, marking lives spent in humiliation and submission.

All around me, and as far as the eye could see, stretched the future in crystal-clear memory that was not mine.

When I finally saw the familiar world of my room, I quickly got dressed and ran out into the bright day. I rushed to the cemetery below the Old Town here in Ulcinj, where I had really buried my grandmother in the presence of two gravediggers and several of her old friends, who in the meantime had also died. Grandmother was buried here on 5th August, not in the winter and not in Bar; not on a squally day but in the suffocating heat; not with indifference but with all the pain I was capable of feeling. The old ladies, her friends, gave speeches and I cried all the way through, which they found touching. Even the gravediggers felt it appropriate to comfort me because I was crying so persistently. I remembered all that. But at the same time I wasn't sure about it all because the memory that gripped me that morning was suddenly purer and more powerful than my own.

I ran to the cemetery in the hope of finding out what I really did remember. I stood in front of my grandmother's grave and heaved a sigh of relief. The gravestone did give her name: Olga Hafner, born 9th May 1930, died 5th August 2003. *Erected by her loving grandson,* was carved in the marble.

12

When I got home, I tipped all the photos of my grandmother onto the floor and started looking through them again, searching for some detail to support the suspicion I was unable to shake off. I went through the family history for myself again and again, like a student preparing for a crucial exam.

Apparently, my mother had ignored my grandmother, who begged her not to go with that man. She fell in love with my father, a good-looking officer, who was a thrice-decorated piece of shit. It was his bravery that killed him. He went to Libya and died there in circumstances that were suspicious, to say the least. When he found out my mother was pregnant, he quit the army and vanished. He was a man who feared no enemy and saved two comrades from a burning tank (his first medal); who boldly intercepted assassins sent into the country by Croatian Ustashi émigrés (his second medal); and who shielded a general with his body when a crazed soldier from Kosovo fired at him (his third medal). And yet he fled head-over-heels from me, who wasn't even born. He heard I was due in five months' time and knew instantly what he had to do. He discarded everything – status, friends and the wife he claimed to love – and moved to Greece, where he enlisted in an American paramilitary outfit. They sent him to Libya, from where he never returned. His name was rarely mentioned in our house. Grandmother made sure of that. She told me terrible tales about that man, so I grew up grateful that I'd never have to meet him.

My mother was killed in a traffic accident in Germany soon after my birth. Grandmother then resigned from her job in the police force, where she worked as an office clerk, and devoted her entire life to me. From Visoko in Bosnia, where I was born, we moved to her family's house in Ulcinj. Her ancestors were originally from Izmir, she told me, and had come to Ulcinj following the Messiah – Sabbatai Zevi. They were in Zevi's company when he and his devotees put ashore at the quay, here at the end of the Ottoman Empire; for the Sultan had banished them when the Messiah's prophecies became too irrational, and the man himself too mad to be bought off and too famous to be executed – thus the danger to the throne. As Jews, this was just another station of exile for them. Zevi died ten years after coming to Ulcinj. His followers remained here to guard his grave, waiting for him to fulfil his prophecy that he would be resurrected. Grandmother told me that her distant ancestor, the one who first raised a house here, on whose ruins ours was built after the 1979 earthquake, was among the chosen ones who lowered Zevi into the earth, from where he had not yet arisen.

Grandmother and I lived together happily in Ulcinj – we needed no one else – until one searingly hot day when a dry sirocco was blowing, and her kind heart failed.

The sorrow I felt in the first few days after her departure and the funeral soon gave way to a sense of complete freedom. There was no one else I loved, and no one else loved me. I was no longer indebted to anyone or anything. My life belonged to me alone, and I didn't give a tuppence for it. There was nothing I desired in the future, and there was nothing in the past that others desired of me that would enslave me. Everything was here and now, doused with alcohol and filled with idleness and indifference. Why delve into the past, when all I would find there could only jeopardize the perfect freedom I lived in?

And then Uncle Tripko spoiled everything in just a few sentences. He seeded doubt in me that I couldn't root out. I had never cared about my background. I was brought up not to ask and not to think about my family. And yet here I was, examining the flimsy, perfunctory saga of a family that lurched from one misfortune to another, a story that suddenly revealed gaping holes and soon turned out to be a fairy tale, shabbily contrived and unconvincingly told. How could I have believed in it, I asked myself, aware of the answer: Because I wanted to. That was enough; that is always enough. Everything we believe in is a fairy tale. The firmness of our belief does not depend on the persuasiveness of the story but on our determination to remain blind to all evidence that could turn the story on its head. If we decide to seek the truth, everything collapses like a house of cards. Truth levels everything before it like an earthquake and carries it away like a flood. As soon as doubt arises, everything is doomed: Nothing remains of all we believed in, happily relied on and made the foundation of our existence – only ruins covered in stinking sludge.

13

Here were the photos I had browsed through with grandmother hundreds of times: Her and my mother drinking coffee beneath a cherry tree in the garden in Visoko one May; her and my mother in Ilica Street in Zagreb, arguing about my father (grandmother with her arm around my mother's shoulders, my mother looking through her, a tram passing by, and an elderly gentleman who had just come out of an ice-cream parlour bowing to them and raising his hat); her and my mother in front of Le Plaza Hotel in Brussels, where they spent two pleasant nights in long conversations about the Magritte exhibition they had seen, with coffee and Petit-Beurre biscuits; her and my mother in Red Lion Square in London, searching for Cromwell's secret grave; her strolling beside Lake Ohrid in an elegant costume bought in Paris; her and friends at a festive lunch at the source of the River Bosna to mark the retirement of her colleague Milutin, who played the accordion and sang Bosnian ballads like a nightingale, and who died of a heart attack not long afterwards while singing like a nightingale to celebrate the birth of a grandson, an event he had waited a whole decade for, saying over and over again, 'I just want to have a grandson, then I can die in peace', meaning he died happy, like a man whose final wish has been granted; her and me strolling along the Stradun promenade in Dubrovnik, where she went with me for my seventh birthday (the bus from Ulcinj took five whole hours); her at the grave of her daughter in the town of Kronberg near Frankfurt, where she bought me a little sailor suit in a children's clothing boutique (I wore that suit obsessively until it fell to pieces – its process of disintegration was recorded in several photos); her at a Munich airport café drinking Julius Meinl coffee with milk and waiting for the clerks of the bank where my mother kept some hard cash she had willed to me (money my grandmother intended to spend on my education but which would be eaten up by the hyperinflation of the 1990s); and her by the sea in Oslo, where she travelled as if to fulfil the desire of one of her daughters, who died without having seen the northern ends of the earth, which she had dreamed of all her life. All these scenes were suddenly no more than illustrations of a tall story to lull a child to sleep. They documented nothing but lies.

But instead of telling myself to stop, I returned the photos to their places in the albums. Instead of shaking off all the questions I had and all that would necessarily follow, because questions are like misfortunes and never come alone, I crammed everything into my rucksack and raced off to Podgorica with the kind of determination that can only get you into trouble fast. Mandušić arranged for me to be received immediately at the forensic centre, where they promised to carry out a full analysis of the 'evidence', as they called it, as quickly as possible.

Needless to say, the findings confirmed my doubts. They are always confirmed.

All the photos were fakes. But very well done, I was told, the work of a master retoucher – a true professional. They were all produced in the same workshop in the space of a few days. It was as if someone had been given the task of fabricating a watertight family history Grandmother hadn't been to Oslo, Germany, London or Brussels, at least not in those photos. She had never argued with my mother in Ilica Street or had a congenial coffee with her in Visoko. Who was that young woman in the photos with her? Who was my mother, Ida Hafner? - And my grandmother? - Was she really mine? - And who the bloody hell am I? So many questions that couldn't be ignored once they had finally been asked...

14

What could I do? I sold the house and moved to Podgorica, where I used the money to buy a flat. The investigation that had been foisted upon me and that I was now in the midst of could not be conducted from Ulcinj. I had to be physically close to the police, whose resources Mandušić generously placed at my disposal.

"What you're telling me requires serious organization and means," he said tersely and called Inspector Todorović, whom he instructed to assist me in any way I needed. "Interesting, very interesting," he muttered. "You'll appreciate that this is now my problem too – having a man close to me with a past like this..."

I took a trip to Visoko, where I was supposedly born and had family roots. There was no proof of my birth there, nor any trace of Olga, Ida or me, David Hafner. But in the local archive I did find a birth certificate and a baptismal record for Tripko Pavlović, who had a sister named Olga.

I travelled on from Visoko to Višegrad and booked into a motel there. That same night, I sneaked out and broke into Tripko's house. I located his photo albums without much trouble. They were full of photos of him and Olga Pavlović, my grandmother.

The next day, already back in Podgorica, I met with Todorović on the terrace of Hotel Montenegro. He had promised to make enquiries with the Bosnian police about Olga Pavlović, and now he read out some of the notes the Sarajevo police had compiled. It turned out that she really had worked as a police clerk in the section that issued identity papers in Hrasno, a suburb of Sarajevo, where she had moved as a teenager and finished high school. Olga was reliable and popular with the other staff members. Her former colleagues stated that they had been surprised when she decided to take early retirement in August 1983, less than four months after I was born. Milutin Zec, who she shared an office with, said that it was 'as if the earth had swallowed her up'. As far as he knew, she never got in touch with any of her co-workers and friends again after she retired. He searched for her at her old address, 103 Lenin Street in the suburb of Grbavica, but the door of her flat was opened by a woman he had never seen before, who had come to the city from some God-forsaken village. She wasn't sure, but she seemed to recall that Olga had mentioned moving to the coast. After that, Zec no longer searched for her, but he hoped for a long time that that kind and cheerful woman would get in touch again one day, when the unusual circumstances that had befallen her and forced her into such secrecy had changed; and he emphasized how 'out of character' her abrupt departure was.

15

Despite these revelations, it took months before I finally made a break-through in the investigation, which seemed to have run up against a tall, impenetrable wall separating me from myself.

Podgorica was sticky and slow. The months there passed like months in hell. Podgorica is a city of false poets, false academics, false journalists, false civil-society activists, false political leaders and false fathers of the nation. The city is a heap of lies and falsehoods on a patch of sun-scorched ground.

And all that is to do with the simple fact that Podgorica is a fake city. I had often mused about there apparently being cities without boulevards, but until I came to Podgorica I didn't know there could be boulevards without a city. To live amidst such haughty ugliness, as one is surrounded with in Podgorica, is unbearable for anyone with an ounce of good taste.

Old Podgorica was destroyed during the Allied bombing raids in 1944. The only way to make the new Podgorica more beautiful would be to conduct a new and equally devastating bombardment.

But the greened terrace of Hotel Montenegro was a comfortable niche in that extremely unwelcoming city, and I had my weekly meetings with Todorović there. Over time, he was sounding increasingly like a scratched record; no progress, no progress, no progress... In the end, he and I talked about everything: football, politics, and alcohol – anything but the job he was meant to be doing for me. Todorović, like all policemen, had the talent of being inconspicuous when he wanted to be, and that is a quality I appreciate in people whose company I share. Our weekly stock of comments on current events would quickly be used up, so we drank our coffee and smoked in silence, watching the passers-by swarm along Saint Peter Cetinjski Boulevard, while liveried waiters darted to and fro around us. They looked like they had stepped out of a time machine that had come straight from the 1980s and the days following Tito's death.

Hotel Montenegro was supposedly a scaled-down replica of a hotel in Havana, so, sitting in the shade of the tall, massive Cuban columns during Podgorica's sweltering heat, you could imagine you were somewhere nicer. The hotel's furnishings were old and functional, in contrast to the leather armchairs and marble tables of Podgorica's other hotels and bars. Here they served strong Turkish coffee and perfect Jelačić cubes, confections named after the former Croatian viceroy that were rich yet refreshing, as well as caramelized-milk ice cream – a flavour full of childhood memories.

The city authorities were no different to the populace of Podgorica in feeling the greatest imaginable antipathy towards beauty and tradition of any kind, and ultimately they ordered that Hotel Montenegro be demolished and a chrome-and-glass Hilton was raised in its place.

When they destroyed the only place in Podgorica where you could feel you weren't in Podgorica, my meetings with Todorović came to an end. They say that Guy de Maupassant vocally opposed the construction of the Eiffel Tower. He claimed it would irreparably destroy Paris. When the tower was built, because progress, particularly progress towards the worse, cannot be halted, journalists observed that Maupassant had the habit of dining in the Eiffel Tower's restaurant. Stupid as journalists always are, they reminded him that he had been the most vocal opponent of the construction of the Eiffel Tower and asked if it wasn't hypocritical for him to now be sitting in the tower every day. "Not at all," he allegedly replied, "the Eiffel Tower is the only place in Paris where you cannot see the Eiffel Tower."

In Podgorica, alas, you always knew you were in Podgorica. A city that, like all other urban abortions in the world, constantly and aggressively reminds you of its existence. I therefore kept my outings to an essential minimum – although it was still unbearable – and received Todorović's empty reports by phone in the flat.

I am a person prone to nostalgia and who can enjoy sorrow. Few things in life have brought me as much happiness.

Cooped up in my flat in Podgorica, I missed the routine of my old life in Ulcinj; the security of repetition and the comfort of rituals. I missed the throng of the steep, narrow lanes, which always had water running down them from the nearby courtyards where women washed carpets and children yelled in a language I had never learned. I missed the old men in their white caps, like egg shells, sitting on stools in front of the pastry shops and smoking, the tinkle of bicycles on the worn-out cobblestones, and the voice of the muezzin from on high, calling the faithful to prayer. I missed the wall of sound on summer afternoons; the hysterical cicadas, the braying of thirsty donkeys and the stomp of horses left to wander the olive groves all summer (in the Autumn they would be taken out to the scrub to cart firewood their owners gathered for sale). I missed the clear February days cleansed by the northeaster, the cold that the wind brings from the snow-covered Albanian hills, a freshness good for thinking and for sleeping. I missed my conversations with Goran, so much like confessions. And, most of all, I missed Maria.

16

She wrote to me. She sent long emails and brilliant essays imbued with her exquisite melancholy, which grew and grew, towering over her like the blue shadow of a tired, old oak, its branches like sonorous, silver gallows. Her thoughts about suicide, which at first frightened her and made her want to dispel them, merged into an idea that took control of her, and she became its fragile body. If I had been able to imagine myself as a knight, even for just one second, I would have raced off to Ulcinj to try and save her. But to love means to unconditionally accept. To love Maria meant to love the death that was approaching not timidly, like a thief in the night, but proudly and with dignity, like a matriarch with her retinue.

My mother hasn't come out of her room for years, she once wrote. *The servants bring food and alcohol to her chambers. Ever less food, ever more drink. They leave the trays at the door and run without looking back; fear drives them, and so they gossip about her in the kitchen. The only sign that she is still alive are the empty bottles and tins they discover from time to time in the corridor. One night I opened my eyes and saw her naked, still beautiful – terrifyingly beautiful – leaning over me in bed. She put her hand on my forehead: "My poor child, my poor little me," she whispered. Her hand was icy cold and as soft as a spider's web. I wanted to speak, but I was only able to stare at her. Then sleep took me.*

17

At the time, Maria was reading Jacques Le Goff's *Your Money or Your Life: Economy and Religion in the Middle-Ages*. Despite her nervous disorder and all the alcohol, her mail to me left no doubt that her intellect was still a fine instrument she played like a virtuoso:

> William of Auxerre wrote on the cusp of the twelfth and thirteenth centuries: 'The usurer acts against the natural laws of the universe because he sells time, which is common to all creatures... nothing gives itself as naturally as time: willy-nilly, all things have time. Since the usurer sells what necessarily belongs to all creatures, he injures all creatures, even the stones; thus, if men were silent against the usurers, the stones would cry out if they could; this is another reason why the Church pursues the usurers.' The usurers misappropriate God's time, with terrible repercussions: earthly justice is curtailed. And, William adds against the usurers: 'God says: *When I take back possession of time, that is, when time is in My hands again and no usurer can sell it, I will judge in accord with justice.*' David, the accusation could not be more serious: the usurers prevent God from administering justice fairly! But if the usurers stole God's time, was the Church not a party to the crime?
>
> The stakes in the conflict between the Church and the usurers were enormous: 'The whole of economic life at the dawn of mercantile capitalism was called into question', Le Goff writes. An enduring ban on earning money based on time, which is the essence of usury, would have meant destroying the very precondition for credit transactions. It would have meant an alternative history. Can we imagine history without banks, without debt?
>
> On one side stood the Church's time, which belonged to God and could not be sold. On the other there was that of the merchants, whose business rested on 'hypotheses around the concept of time – the accumulation of stockpiles in anticipation of scarcity, and buying and selling at favourable moments'.
>
> Our world is at a crossroads. Concession by concession, each of which is more significant than the last, 'the aristocracy of money changers is succeeding the aristocracy of money minters'. In the Middle-Ages, 'a great indifference towards time' prevailed. But after Saint Bernard, who

cursed money, people soon arrived at the conviction that *time is money*: not just subject to sale, but a firm currency that ensures prosperity and social prestige for those who possess and distribute it. All this, Le Goff says, 'heralds the Stock Exchange, where minutes and seconds would create and destroy fortunes'.

In 1355, the councillors in Aire-sur-la-Lys allowed entrepreneurs to erect a belfry, whose bells would not call to prayer but chime the hours of commercial transactions and the working hours of the weavers. The workers who came from the surrounding villages to work needed to be called. The church bells lost their monopoly over the measurement of time. Many contemporaries were concerned and considered that Europe was beginning to beat to "infernal rhythms".

Time therefore became secularized. It would no longer flow to the cadence of divine service but to the rhythms of production and transaction. The merchant who travels in order to open up opportunities for his business and thus extends the market is living Aristotle's definition: *Time is the number of motion.*

He is aware of the price of time; the duration of his journey can be clearly expressed in terms of money.

For the merchant, professional time becomes the time he lives in, a dimension fundamentally detached from petrified, supernatural, ecclesiastical time, whose demands he will ever more be obliged to ignore. But the merchant will donate part of his profit to the Church and work on his own personal salvation. Le Goff says, "It is important to eliminate the suspicion that the psychology of the medieval merchant was hypocritical." He sincerely hoped for salvation, but he prayed with equal sincerity for the success of his transactions, in which he resold *God's time*.

Before long, the citizens of Aire would be calling the time given by the working bell *reliable hours*, as opposed to the *unreliable* hours of the church belfries. The decisive move towards the domination of working time came with mechanical clocks, Le Goff writes. The foundations of that innovation were laid in the thirteenth century, and by the second quarter of the fourteenth century urban clocks had been installed across northern Italy, Catalonia, Flanders, Germany, northern France and southern England. The sixty-minute hour was introduced, which constituted one twenty-fourth of the day. Instead of the working day, which went from dawn till dusk, the so-called *nono*, the ninth hour, was introduced and the hour became the basic unit of work. The ninth hour was intended for rest. It began around what today is two in the afternoon and finished at three, only to be brought forward to today's *noon*. Did you know that that is the origin of the word noon? Despite these developments, time had not yet been standardized. In *Journey to Italy*, Michel de Montaigne describes the chaos a traveller finds himself in because time changes from one city to another: The zero hour is sometimes midnight, sometimes noon, and it could also be sunrise or sunset, Le Goff explains. The crucial shift towards subjectivising time would only come with the invention of the wristwatch, which measures our personal time. It also marked the end of *God's time*.

18

In another letter, Le Goff's book fuelled her obsession with debt and guilt. She wrote to me:

Dear David,

If we've learned anything from Nietzsche, it's that the relationship of the debtor and the creditor is the foundation of society. It's like this: the morals of a community are a catalogue of what we owe others; tradition – of what we owe our ancestors; the family we were born into – what we owe our parents; the Church as steward – what we owe God; patriotism – what we owe the State and nation; the economy – what we owe the usurers; ecology – what we owe Mother Nature; life itself – what we owe God, Nature, providence and chance... or in my case my dear mother, who never fails to remind me of that.

And politics is a guardian of the system where everything can be changed except the fundamental debtor-creditor relationship, i.e. nothing. What then is the meaning of life other than damn repayment of debt? I mean, other than the production of even more debt to saddle our children with? Which you and I won't have, fortunately, because we're not villains like that.

I think I've already mentioned Benjamin's essay to you, the one where he claims capitalism is a pure religious cult – one of the most extreme in human history. A cult is something that turns our lives into an unrestricted celebration of the outwardly secular, but which is actually occult; a permanent liturgy, restless and merciless. It is a cult that, instead of repentance and absolution, offers an endless feeling of guilt that becomes stronger with every heartbeat, an endless accumulation of debt; both ethically and literally, expressed in money. I read in the paper this morning that every French baby comes into the world with 22,000 euros of debt. People are thus born in chains, while all around us, as far as the eye can see, flags of freedom proudly fly. Before the baby grows up and can begin working and repaying the debt, it needs an education. Which is not possible, of course, without incurring additional debt. The Federal Reserve estimates that the total sum of student loans in the USA amounts to one thousand billion dollars.

I know all this, and still *I can't do it...* I can't because I feel a debt to my mother, who had me so I would be her toy, and then kept me to be her slave. I can't, because that debt makes me feel guilty. Benjamin points out that the German word *Schuld* means both guilt and debt.

There is no mouse-hole for me to hide in, not when I'm surrounded by all those stewards of debt acting as agents of the creditor. The Church is the most flagrant example. Jesus died for us on the cross to free us, after which we are indebted exclusively to the Church. It warns us that writing off the debt will not come cheaply – we are indebted to those who represent Him who relieved us of our debts. That is what has now become of La Nona Ora, the ninth hour...

At the ninth hour, Jesus cried out with a loud voice: 'Eloi, Eloi, lama sabachtani?' Father, Father why have you forsaken me? I yell and shout: Mother, Mother why will you not forsake me?

How was that woman able to implant the idea in me that I have no right to kill myself while she is alive? To begin with, she considered the pregnancy from which she bore me to be a greater sacrifice than Jesus' death. Jesus ultimately died at the ninth hour, while she had to carry me for a whole nine months. She preached at me about the pain of parents who lose a child. There was nothing more terrible, she said, and surely I wouldn't do that to my poor mother. She hammered that into my head, so now I hang from the gallows of life, bleeding and in pain, but there will be no relief for me until she dies, which she refuses to do. The tanker loads of alcohol she's drunk would have killed an elephant, but she continues to drink and to rule this house with confidence, along with my life. She is the owner of my debt.

It's like that everywhere, the whole world over. The Academy of Arts and Sciences and other institutions of national culture present themselves as stewards of tradition. The army traditionally figures as a steward of the debt to the nation-state, while in peacetime the class of political representatives assumes that job. Not to mention the Super-ego, which is the most brutal debt collector. However much guilt people feel, and however much regret they pay off the interest with, the principal remains untouched (moreover, the more we regret, the greater the guilt), but the actual amount we owe is unknown, though obviously immeasurable. The issue of debt is evidently a keystone of society, but also of our personality.

The representatives of debt like to stress that we are free. My mother, too, says I should do as I like and tells me it's my life and mine alone. But before I take the final step, I should at least spare a thought for my mother and what it would mean for her... That's how it is. Not only did Jesus free us, but freedoms are also guaranteed to us by the Constitution and the laws of the land, as well as the Charter of Human Rights, libertarian traditions, and ultimately the army, as our freedom's last line of defence. We are free, ultimately, to choose our usurer: The choice of bank where we will raise a loan is a luxury and ours alone.

Whenever I look at my watch, it's three o'clock – always the ninth hour. I wake up at night, drag myself to the kitchen because I'm burning with thirst, and the clock on the wall shows three in the afternoon. Has it stopped? I check, and I see that it's working. Then at dawn, when the mist has fled before the light and those stupid roosters are crowing their heads off, the clock in my mobile shows three in the afternoon. I check all the clocks in the house; they all say it's three. I tell Tereza, the cook, a *woman of the people* and an expert on the irrational. She crosses herself and offers me her rosary. "You need protection, don't refuse The Saviour," she says to me. "I'll pray for you when I'm next at the monastery." She's five months pregnant, but that doesn't stop her from going by bus on a pilgrimage to Ostrog Monastery every third week. What does she pray for there? For the return of her child's father, who bolted when he heard she was pregnant.

19

There were times she would ring at three in the morning, sometimes drunk, sometimes stoned. We'd talk until dawn, or until she fell asleep with the phone in her hand. Then I lay in bed and listened to her breathing. That was all I had of her. It was enough.

20

My days in Podgorica continued like that until Todorović knocked on my door one morning and announced jubilantly: "We're onto something!"

Olga Hafner, actually Olga Pavlović, my grandmother who wasn't my grandmother, had signed a deed of adoption and taken me from an orphanage in September 1983. The manager of the orphanage was still alive. Todorović had found her in Dobrota, near Kotor, where she had retired to a house inherited from her late husband. At first she refused to talk on the topic: "It was so long ago. No one can remember things like that." But Todorović was persistent, and in the end she told him that a secret-service agent had brought the boy to the orphanage. "We'll send someone for him," the gloomy man said before he left. Less than a month later, he visited again and gave her instructions: "The woman will introduce herself as Olga Hafner. This is her photograph. You'll give her the child, and you won't ask any superfluous questions. Is that clear?"

She saw the agent once more – after the woman had taken the baby. He suddenly turned up in her office and sat down at the desk. He demanded all the documents that proved the child had been at the orphanage and then proceeded to burn them one by one. "None of these ever existed," he explained to her. "None of this ever happened, especially not the child. Is that clear?"

She was a woman for whom orders were orders, particularly when they came from the State. She would have taken the secret with her to the grave if Todorović had not turned up and invoked the 'interests of the State'. *The system has come to claim its own, so I will give it its due*, she thought.

But the old woman didn't remember my mother's name. She couldn't have, because she had never known it. Neither the mother nor the child had a name, and none of their particulars had ever been revealed to her. She looked after the child in secrecy and passed it on to Olga Hafner under a cloak of silence. Everything to do with the child was a secret – one she never stopped thinking about and still remembered every detail of today, in advanced old age, when even the faces of her late husband and daughter were fading.

That's good for starters, I thought when I saw out Todorović, who had given me three kisses when he arrived, according to Orthodox custom, and gave me three more when he left, glowing with happiness at the idea that Mandušić might promote him for accomplishing the task so well. *I'm becoming a serious secret*, I thought – *something it's not beneath my dignity to deal with.*

I could forget about grandmother and everything she had told me about myself. Now I had to focus on my mother – the key to the story. Who was 'Ida Hafner' and what was her real name? What did that woman do to earn the dubious privilege of having the Yugoslav secret service take care of her child?

So many questions and not a single answer... I'd think about it all tomorrow, I decided. I phoned Goran. As I expected, he accepted my invitation for a party at my place in Podgorica that night. He promised to bring Maria. I had reason to celebrate. Todorović's discovery amounted to an ontological promotion. I wasn't actually a lazy, nihilistic alcoholic from a provincial backwater. Whatever I finally discovered myself to be would be more exciting than what I thought I knew about myself. The feeling that had accompanied me from the very beginning of my existence – a sense of absolute, cosmic coldness and solitude – now seemed much more complex than a whim or a character flaw; it seemed understandable, justified and ultimately correct. Not only did I perceive all my fellow citizens as foreign, but I was a foreigner to myself. That's how it was and that's how it always would be, because that's how it was meant to be.

I opened a present from Mandušić – a bottle of eighteen-year-old Jura, poured myself three fingers of whisky (the closest I ever got to Orthodoxy and their three-finger salute) in a crystal glass of my grandmother's; stretched out on the couch and put on a Mono album at full blare: *For my Parents.*

21

The party was to my liking, lots of alcohol and not many people. I had a load of Mandušić's whisky all to myself because Maria and Goran were getting into a batch of rare Primitivo Barrique – no more and no less than ten bottles – that they had taken from Elletra's splendid wine cellar. Everything was great until Radovan turned up with two business partners and a prostitute in tow.

You could see straight way that he had succeeded in life. The lady of his heart had rags worth a good two thousand euros *on* her and at least twice that much *in* her, in implants. I congratulated Radovan on moving on from *The Second Chance* and those asylum seekers from undemocratic Eastern Bloc states, and I really meant it – I am someone who takes delight in others' good fortune. But that wasn't to the liking of his escort. She claimed she wasn't a prostitute; in any case she didn't feel like one. Seething with rage, she stepped up to me and hit me with her CV. She had earned a law degree and gained a PhD in public relations; now she ran an NGO that 'worked to strengthen democratic institutions and control the work of the Montenegrin government in co-ordination with a number of foreign embassies in Podgorica' – those were her exact words; and she performed legal services for Radovan in connection with a site he had bought in Bar, where he planned to develop a five-star, luxury boutique hotel. She had come along because Radovan insisted and assured her I wasn't a bad guy, although she harboured the deepest contempt for me as well as all intellectuals who betrayed every principle they had ever stood for.

Radovan grabbed her by the hand and pulled her away to the other room, where, to my horror, he poured her a full glass of Mandušić's whisky. Then he came back to me and said with a wink: "How about she blows you one afterwards? I'll pay."

"No thanks," I said. "That bit about co-operating with foreign embassies hit me like a ton of bricks. I hate to think what that means and what repercussions it could have for the people of this country, and thus for me. Call it paranoia if you like, but after that I need a good stiff drink," I remarked and walked away. I hoped I'd seen the last of him.

Throughout the evening, Radovan and his business partners took it in turns to perform legal consultations with the NGO activist in my toilet and showed absolutely no interest in mixing with me, Goran and Maria. The three of us went out onto the balcony and sat there, drinking. Maria and I were slagging off Radovan, who, ever since we'd known him, had succeeded in turning other people's money into his own and setting up a big construction firm that sold hundreds of flats along the coast. Like me, Maria had detested him from the very beginning but put up with him because he found it 'awesome' to socialise with us and was willing to be our free taxi service and drive us home when we were drunk, high or sick. Now Maria, like me, didn't have the nerves to cope with this animal any more. Goran, as usual, had to say a few words in his defence. That struck me as suspect.

"Hold on, you haven't become a 'business partner' of Radovan's too, have you?"

He went red. The topic was clearly unpleasant for him. He decided to play the, *I'm offended that you even thought of it* card. I didn't want to torment my friend, so I accepted his bluff:

"Forget it, I was just joking. They're all welcome. Cheers, and may our livers always be young..."

The peaceful coexistence between Radovan's crew and us lasted until Maria wanted to dance and put on 'Enola Gay' by Orchestral Manoeuvres in the Dark.

"Why the hell did ya put on those poofs?" the drunken Radovan yelled the moment he heard the word *gay*.

I opened the door and pointed to the corridor.

"Out!" I hissed. "Or would you prefer leaving through the window?"

Those swine who had rooted their way to success in the new capitalist system figured I meant business. They were right, animals like that have a good sense of danger. They grabbed their things and made a move, leaving a few used condoms behind on my bathroom floor.

"You're making a mistake, mate," Radovan whispered on the way out. "Things have changed – you're not in a position to mess around Radovan any more."

I slammed the door behind them.

"Good, let's start again," I called, as if they had never been there. "Put the song on again."

That was just what Maria had been waiting for. I dropped into the armchair and watched as she danced with her eyes closed, so beautifully, with such dedication, as if that was her last will and testament, as if she had chosen it to be her life's final deed.

Later, when Maria had fallen asleep on the couch and Goran and I were pouring our third *one more and then it's off to bed* out on the balcony, I explained what had so infuriated me about Radovan's idiotic comment.

"What you don't know is that that song is my and Maria's little secret," I told him. "Once we were sitting on the terrace of my house in Ulcinj before dawn, after a drinking spree that makes this look tame, watching the calm sea and the currents coming up from Otranto, and she proposed a scenario for the end of the world. Imagine - shit happens and everything is obliterated in the flood. Only she and I survive. Nothing terrible, you might say; we are the new Adam and Eve, and everything can begin anew. But then we give the 'up yours' salute to God, history and the human race. We live happily and not particularly long. But we never shag and make babies, so everything ends with us. The two of us reign over a world, finally globalized, where only two human beings still exist and there is only one state – ours. And its anthem is 'Enola Gay'."

"Why did Maria choose that of all songs? 'Enola Gay' isn't a pro-gay hit from the 1980s, as Radovan thought, and as the former BBC1 editors also assumed when they banned it from being aired. Enola Gay was the name of the plane that dropped the atom bomb on Hiroshima. Enola Gay was also the name of the pilot's mother. Imagine, he named the B-29 *Superfortress* that would sow fire and death after his mother! 'What dedication to the mother-destroyer! What a man! What a son!' Maria exclaimed in a rapture of delight, I told him.

Goran patted me on the shoulder and trudged inside. I heard him crash onto the bed.

I poured myself another whisky and stared at the empty streets that Maria and I would reign over with composure one day when everything was finished, when the water receded and the sludge it left behind dried, and the bones of those it had purged from the world were crumbled by the sun and blown away by the wind. My queen slumbered in her chamber while I, the tired ruler, stood a lonely vigil over my kingdom.

22

Two years passed, and still I knew nothing more about my mother – and thus about myself. I was still cooped up in my hole in Podgorica. One time Mandušić tried to pull me out of there. An international meeting was being held in Budva, where the participants were to use lofty terms such as 'democracy', 'human rights' and 'united Europe' to explain why complete control of the population was necessary. Mandušić imagined *I* could attend as a speaker for the Montenegrin police.

I agreed because the meeting was to be held at *Hotel Splendid*, and I saw the opportunity for a free binge and for enjoying the luxurious rooms and bars.

I had planned to write my speech there, in Budva. But I stayed up late drinking on the first night of the conference, and the second as well. On the third day, I decided to talk without a prepared speech. I went up to the rostrum in front of around a hundred police, politicians and activists, and told them the following story.

Several years ago I met Peter, a Hungarian writer, in a beachside café in Ulcinj. I don't know what he was doing there. But, as usual when I run into a foreigner wandering our country and desperately searching for a way out of the labyrinth of ugliness and mindlessness they have voluntarily entered, I felt a sense of shame – as if I was somehow to blame for their misfortune.

Peter was a great guy. He was a misanthrope, but those are the only kind of people who should be allowed to enter Montenegro, where only misanthropes will feel at home and find everything they're looking for.

Before I could finish my first espresso, he let fire three politically incorrect, and therefore witty, remarks.

"Is it true that Russians have bought up half of Montenegro?" he asked.

"They do literally buy territory, and no one knows how much of the country they already own," I told him. "Montenegrins are satisfied for the time being. They sell land to the Russians, buy flats and big SUVs, and then drive along the coast and bellyache about the Russians having bought everything. On the way they tank up their fuel-guzzling jeeps at Russian-owned Lukoil petrol stations. Soon all the petrol stations are going to be Russian, people say, because allegedly Lukoil is going to purchase Jugopetrol. Montenegro previously sold it to the Greeks, but they're unable to make a buck even from selling petrol."

"What's the solution then?" Peter asked me.

"The solution is universal and always the same," I told him. "In the end, the Montenegrins will stage a revolution, nationalize everything, and then things will start all over again. Or they won't. But that's always an option."

Then Peter, who had now drunk four espressos and moved on to Jägermeister, began a nostalgic colonial discourse.

"Hungary used to have access to the sea," he told me. 'The Adriatic was our *mare nostrum* and Pula – the traditional summer resort for Hungarians. We built Rijeka, and even Naples was once ours."

One of the effects of coffee consumption must be the annulment of colonial consciousness, it occurred to me.

Then our conversation moved on to suicide.

"The suicide rate in Hungary has always been high," Peter told me. He was one of those people where you can't tell from their face if they're being deadly serious or lucidly sarcastic. "People from elsewhere misinterpret the Hungarians' predilection for suicide. In Hungary, suicide isn't to do with depression. It's a culturological phenomenon, above all. Hungarians are a proud people who love their freedom. To die on your own terms, at a time of your choosing, is the only true freedom."

"Listen, Peter, it looks to me as if you Hungarians are the ideal occupiers," I confided in him. "If you get into gear while we're driving out the Russians, you could occupy Montenegro. You'd come, build some roads and other infrastructure, and then simply vanish – by killing yourselves. We wouldn't even have to chase you out."

It dawned on me that a true, mature democracy is not one that guarantees a transition of power without civil war and insurrection, or where minorities are adequately represented in parliament through their own elected delegates. Nor is it one with a complete separation of powers, or where the full rule of law has been achieved, or that successfully uses all legal means of repression in the fight against corruption...

A true, mature democracy is one where the citizens confide responsible public functions solely to people prone to suicide.

To my mind, the story was short, clear and instructive; what else do you expect of a speech?

For some reason the audience didn't share my opinion. There was no applause, not even of the polite, half-hearted variety. People whom I had expected to have seen and heard everything, so that nothing could surprise them any more, looked at me in astonishment, as if I was standing there naked, at the very least. Unable to conceal her uneasiness, the moderator muttered something about it being democratic to listen, even to bizarre and extreme opinions, and hastily called up the next speaker.

I judged that my participation in the conference was no longer required, so I checked out at the hotel reception, gave a generous tip to the young fellow who drove the car up from the garage, and shot off to Podgorica and my flat, which I hated, but at least I wasn't surrounded by idiots there.

23

The media scandalized the whole thing, but two days later everyone forgot about it because a man in Nikšić killed a neighbour and his three small children, so the masses had a new incident to be horrified at. Mandušić didn't comment on the event. He didn't send me to any more meetings like that, though, or to any at all.

But he didn't sack me. It seemed that listeners liked the speeches I wrote for him more than they appreciated my ad libbing in Budva.

He cut my pay by a third, but I didn't complain. It was easily earned money. After sending the first few speeches to Mandušić I realized it was pointless to invest any effort or inventiveness in the work. Everything politicians said and all they were expected to say was a pile of commonplace and mind-numbing phrases. Therefore I prepared about fifty stock sentences; about parliamentary democracy, the inclusion of minority groups, the importance of a military deterrent for the stability of tolerant societies, the history of Montenegro with emphasis on the so-called Mediterranean foundations of its culture, about multiculturalism, a few quotes from Hegel and a little Plato from *The Republic*. I arranged all this on a large, B1 sheet of paper and pinned it to the wall of my study.

It resembled the magic squares the alchemists used to draw in the Middle-Ages. A magic square enchanted the people of the time, just as they have always been fascinated by short sequences containing some pattern, which they like to believe proves the logical order of that large sequence, the biggest one of all, which they call the world. In an alchemist's magic square, the sum of the numbers along the vertical and the diagonal was always the same. In my magic square, however I arranged the hackneyed sentences and whatever order I assembled them in, the effect was the same: Absolute bureaucratic dimness and liberal-democratic ideological blinkering. Applause for the thinker, please. That's the crux of it - people once strove for perfection: Now we're quite satisfied with the least bad of all systems, as its devotees describe democracy.

24

Maria and I started falling out of touch. Like a nugget of gold thrown into water, she sank into melancholy. She went down wordlessly, without resistance, and accepted it as her destiny, if what we are frolicking towards can be called that. Maria's sorrow was more than just a state of mind – it was her own aesthetic choice. Sorrow is so beautiful, she used to tell me, and she only said what she meant. And did what she said.

Goran got a job at a bank. He became a loans officer and felt he had it good. He bought a new car, helped his father repair the roof and do up the front of the house, and generously supported his sister. Our drinking sprees became a rarity and later ceased altogether, because Goran decided that alcohol must not get in the way of his career. So his career got in the way of our friendship, which continued to be as sincere as before – except that we no longer practiced it.

As for my investigation, it really 'got off the ground', as the journos like to say, when I received an email from an unknown address, wovenhand@gmail.com, drawing my attention to the unusual biography of Júlia Fazekas. I read the life-story of this serial killer with interest and enjoyment but then forgot about it. Two weeks later, from the same address, I received what was supposedly a scan of police records compiled by an Inspector Rešid Spahić from the Bosnian Centre for Public Security in Sarajevo.

Spahić claimed to have discovered irrefutable evidence that some of the atrocities committed in Višegrad during the war by a unit under the command of the cousins Milan and Sredoje Lukić had not actually been war crimes as qualified by the tribunal in The Hague, but ritual killings. Spahić assumed there had been more such crimes in Bosnia, and he also suspected that the killers were still at large. And not only that, he maintained that because of the nature of the crimes, because occult killers don't stop until they're arrested, the investigation was bound to reveal a series of murders extending until today. We were dealing with a well-organized group of psychopaths with influence in the State and police apparatus – influence sufficient to block the investigation and send it in the wrong direction – which had left a bloody trail and an unknown number of victims all through the country.

In the first months of the war 1,760 people were killed in Višegrad, hundreds of houses burned down and the mosques demolished. Almost two thirds of the population were forced to flee. Long lines of Muslims left the town, and afterwards Višegrad was proclaimed Serbian. Day after day, for weeks, people were killed and their bodies thrown from the bridge into the Drina. On 18th June, a group under the command of Milan Lukić killed twenty-two people. They were tied to cars and dragged through the town, and parts of their bodies rolled along the streets. Survivors later testified that some of the victims had their throats cut, and then their internal organs removed. Spahić claimed he had discovered a house with a shrine, where those organs were offered to the devil. He claimed to have witnesses, whose identity he wasn't prepared to reveal, as well as photographs confirming his testimony.

On 28th June 1992 – St Vitus' Day and the anniversary of the Battle of Kosovo – Milan and Sredoje Lukić forced about sixty Muslims into a house in Pionirska Street and threw in grenades. Then they set the house on fire. Some people tried to escape by jumping out of the windows, but the Lukićs were waiting outside, armed with automatic weapons, and mowed down the fugitives. They killed fifty-nine people that day. Seventeen of them were children, one of whom had been brought to the house after being born at the maternity hospital the day before. One of the survivors told Spahić that he had seen pentagrams painted in blood on the walls of the house when he was taken there. Later he managed to climb out through the bathroom window and run away before the Lukićs closed off that escape route too, with a hail of bullets. Before his flight from the bathroom he had seen the dismembered bodies of three children and their hearts lying in the bath. He could still see those three little hearts before his eyes today and hear them beating, Spahić's witness said.

I called Todorović. I asked him to enquire about Spahić and try to confirm the authenticity of his report. He came to see me that same afternoon. Yes, Inspector Rešid Spahić did exist. And yes, he had presented his theory about occult crimes in wartime Višegrad to senior staff at the Bosnian Centre for Public Security. It was dismissed as being just another of the conspiracy theories, which Spahić, as it turned out, rather bombarded his superiors with. But he seems to have been particularly fond of this story because he threatened to 'go public' with it if the directors of the Centre didn't agree to open an investigation and grant him the extra powers he was requesting. He was suspended.

He went for a long walk on the slopes of Mount Trebević near Sarajevo, from which he didn't return. His body was never found.

A person unknown to me was trying to tell me something. I assumed I would receive more messages from wovenhand@gmail.com in the days ahead. The sender obviously wanted to direct my attention to something. It was up to me to discover what.

What was the link between the biography of Júlia Fazekas and the Satanists who masked their crime in Višegrad as a war crime?

Who could my mysterious benefactor be? Todorović hadn't been able to pick up his trail, although I explicitly demanded that of him. Police documents were not accessible to just anyone. If he was a member of the police, or someone who controlled its operations, he would be able to find out all the things I got Todorović to ask his friends from the Bosnian services. It could be someone with an interest in me finding out more. Or a person afraid I'd find out something I shouldn't, and who therefore set a trap for me and hoped I'd fall into it.

25

In my efforts to arrive at some answer to these questions, even an inconclusive one, I returned to the biography of Júlia Fazekas, which my mysterious friend had so kindly recommended to me.

Júlia Fazekas was vilified after her death. Today she would be glorified as a radical feminist.

Little is known about her life prior to 1911, when like an angel of death, she appeared in the Hungarian village of Nagyrév, about a hundred kilometres from Budapest. She was a middle-aged widow. The police first took an interest in Júlia in 1911, when an investigation into illegal abortions she had performed did not result in any conviction. Júlia would find herself in court nine more times over the next ten years, faced with the same charge. She was acquitted every time.

When the Great War began, the men of Nagyrév were drafted into the army. The women remained alone – that is, until a prison camp for Allied soldiers was set up near Nagyrév. How exactly they managed it is not known, but the women of Nagyrév arranged for prisoners to come and spend nights in their beds.

Problems began when the menfolk started coming home from the war. Their wives, who had got to know the charms of free love and life outside the fetters of patriarchy, were not willing to go back to the old ways. And that is where Júlia Fazekas helped them.

Júlia had a sizeable supply of arsenic and also of *know-how*, as people would say today. She selflessly shared both with her sisters.

The first victim was called Peter Hegedusz. No one remembers the names of the others who were killed – and it seems there were three hundred of them. This would allow us to conclude that the most important man in a woman's life is not the first one she sleeps with, as is mistakenly believed, but the first one she kills.

To be fair, the sisters didn't just kill men. They also eliminated women who reminded them of their former lives of misery; mothers, sisters, aunts and others.

Júlia Fazekas was the informal village doctor, by fortunate circumstance, so it was she who carried out the post-mortems, if they can be called that. And there was no end to the fortunate circumstances – her cousin was the local clerk in charge of issuing death certificates.

In Júlia's opinion, the men of Nagyrév died a natural death. For fifteen years, the menfolk of that Hungarian village dropped like flies – the result of wartime stress, it seemed – before officials started to get suspicious.

When this brood of vipers had killed off their husbands and male relatives, the sisters got the urge to do a bit of killing in the neighbouring villages, too. In July 1929, a choirmaster from Tiszakürt accused the wife of a certain Ladislav Szabó of trying to poison him with wine. The authorities didn't react – where would they be if they had to follow up every case of intemperance followed by nausea and vomiting in Hungary? But when the fellow dragged himself to the police station, more dead than alive and started shouting in a delirium that Mrs Szabó had poisoned him, they had no choice.

They arrested the lady, and she opened her soul to them. Her testimony led the police to Mrs Bukenoveski. She told them that Júlia Fazekas had provided the arsenic used to kill her seventy-year-old mother in 1924. She threw the body in the River Tisza, and Júlia Fazekas pronounced the old woman dead by drowning.

Eight women from Nagyrév were sentenced to death and seven to life imprisonment. Eleven more were sent to jail. One of these, Mária Szendi, declared in court that she killed her husband because she was fed up with everything always having to be his way. 'It's terrible that men have all the power,' she told the judge, who showed no understanding for her form of struggle for gender equality.

Júlia Fazekas eluded male power and its institutions. She drank a mug of wine laced with her own arsenic.

26

I drew a parallel between Júlia's killings and the 'Višegrad crimes' pointed out by Spahić. These, too, were committed in wartime and went undetected at first. For those with killing in mind, war is the best time. Submerged in a sea of blood and surrounded by so much other killing, crimes committed in wartime have a good chance of going unnoticed. Some set of statistics would show them in the end, but they would most likely be included in the long list of war crimes, just as Spahić claimed.

I needed to go for a walk to air my mind. I headed off along Saint Peter Cetinjski Boulevard towards Podgorica's Block 5, which I passed through without noticing the monstrosity of that Socialist-era estate built for teachers from the villages and the workers of the aluminium smelter. I cut through the leafy Tološi neighbourhood and continued on towards agreeable Mareza, only to find myself the very next moment in Oxford Street, London. I didn't feel a bit of surprise or slow my step. As if they had a will of their own, my legs led me on to Red Lion Square.

I sat down at one of the plastic tables at the small café at the entrance to the park. A Moroccan family – a father and his two teenage daughters – were serving couscous, tahini and soup with meatballs and cinnamon. I wasn't hungry. I ordered mint tea. Smoking cigarette after cigarette, I drank a whole pot of tea, and then ordered another. The head of the family came over to me and sat down at the table. He claimed to know me, and that I had been his guest once before. As far as he could remember, I had slept at the October Gallery, in a comfortably appointed apartment the size of a matchbox located just around the corner.

"You asked me to tell you about Cromwell, remember?" he asked. "You were fascinated by the story about the publican, a follower of Cromwell's, who hid the leader's body from soldiers here on the square. When Cromwell was buried in Westminster Abbey in 1658, he gave them the body of an unknown man he had dug up at the paupers' cemetery. So when the Royalists decided to desecrate Cromwell's tomb in 1660 and take revenge on his remains, it was actually quite a farce for those who knew the secret; the body they dug out of the Westminster tomb, clapped in chains and posthumously beheaded wasn't Cromwell. Do you remember? You wrote down what I told you in a blue notebook with a golden emblem on the cover, just like the one poking out of your rucksack. That's how I remembered you – it's not every day that someone listens to the story about the hidden grave as if it was the greatest secret in the universe. More tea?" he asked as he shook my hand and apologized for having to leave me. "Work calls."

Feeling poisoned by all the nicotine, I walked to the other end of the Square, passing a Korean, who must have been a singer and was posing in a white shirt for a photographer and his numerous assistants. I jumped the fence and headed to the left. I strolled into the Conway Hall as if I was a regular there, passing workers unloading old pianos from a truck. There was no one at the reception. Just like last time, I thought. I went up the winding stairs to the second floor, where, as I expected, I found the door of an office with the sign 'Istros Books - Independent Publishing House'. I went down to the first floor and sat on the balcony of the hall where I remembered watching – or someone else remembered watching – Slavoj Žižek and Srećko Horvat talk about the future of the European Union. The hall was now full of pianos that would soon be sold by auction; a monthly event at the Conway Hall.

I went down a badly lit corridor, passing the office where the person whose memory this was had spoken with an urbane old lady, an intimate friend of Lucian Freud's, and heard her story about the New Year's Eve party where she and Lucian danced. And then I left the building and bought a box of Walker's shortbread at the corner shop. Wandering aimlessly westwards and enjoying the sweet, buttery taste at the top of my mouth, I chanced upon the Wallace Collection.

The poster at the entrance announced that Dürer's *Melencolia I* was on exhibit. An anonymous buyer had apparently acquired the copperplate for 72,500 pounds at Christie's and later decided to donate it to the Wallace Collection, a museum that had played an important role in his life, he confided to the management.

Dürer was on show as 'Treasure of the Month'. Despite that pompous billing, the public didn't care much for the German genius. As in every other gallery or museum, they thronged in front of the Dutch Masters, who were more popular in England than all other painters except Turner, I was so bold as to presume, not knowing if I was presuming it now or back then. The Dutch Masters reminded people of Gobelin tapestries with their quaint or bucolic scenes, except that Gobelins were somehow more cheerful, without the unnecessary dark tones the Dutch plastered their canvases with.

I arrived in front of *Melancholy* in the middle of a presentation. I – for my memory tells me it was I – was now standing beside a curator and two old men, who were crying and holding each other's hands. What a brilliant curator, I thought (now, when I'm remembering this, or back in the gallery?). He was better, in fact, than most of the cultural commentators whose books I used to waste my time on. He spoke with a devotion and passion that are rare today, and which here in the Balkans are only found in zealots who elaborate to people with the same mind-set the reasons for attacking a neighbouring village with murder in mind.

"As Klibansky, Panofsky and Saxl correctly emphasize," the curator explained in a steady voice, "Dürer develops the idea of Geometria succumbing to Melancholy and Melancholy inclined towards Geometria. He unites two figures in this picture: The brilliant mind of Geometria and the destructive seductiveness of Melancholy... Panofsky claims elsewhere that this is actually a spiritual self-portrait of Dürer himself".

The curator then turned our attention to the magic square in the upper right-hand corner of the engraving. The artist's contemporaries, he explained, considered the harmony of the magic square, whose numbers always give the same result, regardless of their arrangement, to symbolize the harmony of the Creator's works.

To my mind, however, the key to understanding the picture was the scrawny dog lying sprawled at Melancholy's feet. In it, I saw the figure of the cynic, that dog among people. Surrounded by all manner of paraphernalia for measuring and discovering the laws of the universe, oppressed by numbers and geometric patterns, disillusioned by both people and angels, he no longer has the strength to warn about the madness of so-called wisdom. He lies there with indifference, waiting for everything to collapse and for that which he rationally warned about to be confirmed, which the others just heard as a bark.

But I didn't stop in front of Dürer for long because my attention was attracted to a pen-and-ink drawing to the left of Melancholy. It showed a barefoot man in tatters, accompanied by an old woman in rags. The figures were represented in a realistic manner. The burdens they carried on their backs clearly set their existence apart from the sublime Melancholy. I forgot about Dürer and devoted all my attention to studying the symbols the artist had placed around his two sad heroes. The barren tree could represent winter, but I preferred to see it as a genealogical dead end; a withered and poisoned family tree, which all the names had fallen from like yellow leaves. The old woman warmed herself at a brazier, which revealed her vocation - it was an accessory for black magic. A piece of parchment with a hexagram and other magical symbols lay on the ground next to her. From that woman, his mother, there was no escape.

"The owl you see –," I heard the curator's voice, and turned around towards him, noticing that we were now alone in the hall, with him standing unusually close to me, 'does not just symbolize night, solitude and ill omen. Here, too, we profit greatly from Klibansky, Panofsky and Saxl, without whose work no serious interpretation of *Melencolia I* and Dürer's imitators would be possible. They point out that the owl also stands for *studio d'una vana sapienza*, vain wisdom, which is precisely what the Church Fathers accused goddess Minerva's winged servant of. Now look at the cobweb. In the Renaissance, the spider's weaving was considered *opera vana*, labour in vain. That's right, all the labour of the man in the picture is in vain. He is totally under the power of this femme fatale, and that he will remain. All he can do is resign himself – to her and to melancholy."

"The author of this mid-sixteenth-century drawing was a German, perhaps from southern Germany, perhaps from Switzerland; sometimes the work is mistakenly considered French. What attracted me to it, and the reason I devoted a considerable amount of effort to having it here in the complementary collection of Dürer's followers' works, is a seemingly minor detail; the hedgehog. Just look at the cute little creature, which has made its nest right in the barrel the melancholic person is sitting on. Did you know that the female hedgehog keeps putting off the birth of her babies for fear that their spines could tear open her womb? The longer she waits, of course, the bigger and sharper the spines will be, and the greater the pain – that's the price of procrastination. That's how it is with melancholic people, too. Whatever they intend to do, their inhibitions prevent them from doing it and they keep putting it off. But some things just need be done. The melancholic person therefore has to do them in the agony that comes at the end, after all the delay. Think about that," the curator said, patting me on the shoulder and then disappearing into the labyrinth of the Wallace Collection's rooms.

27

When I came round, it was night-time. I was sitting on a beer crate beside the main road to Nikšić with a circle of cigarette butts around me, ten or so kilometres from home. I felt a terrible weariness. With the greatest effort I raised my hand to hail a taxi.

After that, I snored away on the back seat. The angry driver woke me up when we arrived at the address I had managed to mutter. As if I was hauling a whole foreign life behind me, I trudged to the lift, which took me up to my flat. Instead of immediately going to bed, I sat down in front of the television and goggled at a horrendous political debate, where a pack of dim-witted reprobates in the studio were trying to convince the dim-witted viewers to vote for them. This concentrated idiocy shook me awake, and in that tired and irritable state I waited for morning.

My body ached as if someone had been thrashing me all night. Sluggish and half-asleep, I made coffee, sat down at the computer, opened the search engine and typed in 'murders at Red Lion Square'. Nothing. Then I typed 'death at Red Lion Square'. I opened a short newspaper article from 1980, which told me that a certain Jovan Plamenac, aged sixty, fell asleep at the wheel of his car, broke through the fence on Red Lion Square and crashed into a tree. He died at the scene of the accident. The report was accompanied by a small photo of the deceased.

Jovan Plamenac, I found out when I searched further, was a prominent figure in Chetnik émigré circles in London. He had joined Draža Mihailović's Serbian quisling movement as a young man and was rapidly promoted, owing to his cruelty towards the enemy. After the war, he fled via Slovenia to London. The Yugoslav authorities tried Flamenac *in absentia* for the shooting of twelve Partisans in central Serbia, where he had been commander. He was sentenced to life imprisonment. The British authorities refused to extradite him.

From the moment I began to doubt my origins up until that day, the only pattern in my investigation was that nothing was as it seemed. By the same logic, I could assume that Plamenac's death had not been an ordinary traffic accident, either.

Let's say Plamenac was killed. Poisoned, for example, like Júlia Fazekas's victims, and that his death was later attributed to the wrong cause as with Júlia's victims, and with those Inspector Spahić wrote about in his report. How did that relate to my mother and me? The conclusion was improbable, alarming and unwelcome, but inescapable: What if my mother had killed Plamenac, and she did it in such a way to make it look like an accident? Why would she have done that? Why did the Yugoslav secret service take care of her child, me, then give me a false mother, the police clerk Olga Pavlović, and a false identity with the surname Hafner? Was it because my mother worked and killed for the Service? And the Service looked after its own people? That meant that, by my very birth, I had become part of the Service. Is that why Mandušić employed me and tolerated my frankly disgraceful behaviour?

I shared my doubts with Todorović. He looked visibly uneasy while I was speaking and could hardly wait for me to finish.

"You're crazy, quite crazy. Where you're heading is just madness," he said. "Stop before it's too late," he added and left in a hurry.

Something told me my contact with Todorović had come to an end.

That was no longer important. The *crazy* story I had discovered, or constructed – I still had to find out which – needed to be resolved. I got myself an express British visa and took a plane to London, where the trail led.

28

Fuck this for a joke, I thought when I sat down at the Moroccan café on Red Lion Square. I ordered mint tea and lit a cigarette. I must have been really been staring at the Moroccan, because he came up to me.

"Do we know each other?" he asked politely.

"No, not at all," I replied. "Forgive me. You see, a friend told me about you."

"Say hello to your friend," he chuckled and was about to go back to the kitchen to make more food for the guests who were coming in droves now it was lunch hour. I decided to play the game to the end and beckoned him to take a seat.

"I see things are hectic –," I apologized, "but I have to ask, where exactly on this square was Cromwell buried?"

A minute or two later, I came across the piano carriers in front of Conway Hall. I followed the winding stairs up to the second floor and peeked into the office of Istros Books. A blonde woman was working at a computer: "Hello, can I help you?" she asked. Then I went down one floor and took a photo of the pianos that were here to be auctioned.

It suddenly occurred to me that I could visit all the places I had seen in my visions and take photos. That way I could take control of my memory, and also of time. These photos would guarantee that it was *my* memory of *my* time. Later, by comparing my own memories with others' memories of the same places, I would try to discover some kind of trail to follow. Where would it lead me? Probably nowhere, but what else could I do? In my situation, every move, however crack-brained it was, seemed an equally rational choice.

I stayed the night at the October Gallery. The rooms were indeed comfortably appointed and the size of a matchbox.

29

I travelled to London once more that year, too.

The trip came after the birth of an idea that was truly bizarre, but as such not far from the truth. And that idea, in turn, came after another email from Wovenhand.

He had sent me a link to an article about the murder of Stjepan Djureković, one of the Croatian managers of the Yugoslav State oil company INA until he came into conflict with the country's Communist leadership. He fled to Germany and there, seeking safety from his powerful enemy and any allies he could find, he joined up with the Ustashi émigrés. In Yugoslavia he was accused of plundering INA in league with the German secret police.

Djureković was killed in 1983 in the town of Wolfratshausen near Munich. The German media immediately blamed the Yugoslav secret service. They claimed the plan to kill him was code-named 'Operation Danube'. That brought an involuntary smile to my lips. I thought back to my school years and the Geography lessons with a senile teacher, whose name was Melisa. She had a habit of eating chocolate in class and ended every lesson with digressions on the Thracians and Illyians. The Thracians called the lower course of the Danube, which flows through the Balkans, Istros.

I gazed at the article I had been sent. It was old hat. I had already made the connection between my mother and political murders by the Yugoslav secret service without Wovenhand's assistance. So what was my secret friend trying to tell me? Maybe he didn't mean to tell me anything new. Perhaps he just wanted to confirm my doubts and encourage me to keep developing my conspiracy theory.

One mystery still begged to be solved: Olga Pavlović's photos. What was the point of all those trips she never went on? Why all those fake destinations? Why didn't they simply take a pile of photos in Ulcinj? Especially since it was rather unlikely that my make-believe grandmother, who lived modestly and taught me modesty, could have had the money for all those trips abroad. What if the Service itself had left a trail on those photos that they expected me to find, I suddenly thought?

What if I was expected to investigate the locations on those photos?

I sat down at the computer and started an extensive search. By evening I had linked all the places in Olga's photos with the bizarre deaths of members of the Yugoslav diaspora.

At the end of it, I believed Olga's photos were a secret map of the political murders ordered by the Yugoslav secret service. Murders that I now believed – couldn't *not* believe when faced with the evidence – had been committed by my mother.

Independent investigations in the different countries had declared that the deaths were due to 'natural causes' or 'accidents'. But I no longer had any doubt as to what Wovenhand wanted to tell me through those emails. By now I was able to recognize the murderous signature of my mother, who was evidently a virtuoso of death, a master assassin who went undetected, although the murders took place under the very nose of the police.

A pre-war banker and post-war financier of the Ustashi émigrés, who had returned to Zagreb in his old age when he thought he was no longer important to anyone and that no one would want to take revenge on him any more, who had hoped to spend the evening of his life in the city where he was born, was found dead in his flat in Ilica Street.

Then there was a Kosovar, the owner of several patisseries in Brussels, who died in a room of Le Plaza Hotel, where he had checked in accompanied by an eye-catching lady, whom the receptionist didn't doubt was a prostitute – a lady who disappeared without a trace before the police arrived. The investigation confirmed the obvious; that the gentleman suffered a heart attack while having sex. It had been too much excitement for him. He should have borne that in mind, because his medical record card noted that he had had a serious heart condition for many years.

Then there was a poet who, after his works were translated into French, believed he was important and went on to complain to the Paris newspapers about the lack of democracy in his native country, after which he was recruited by the French secret service. Wordsmiths are naturally rapturous, and therefore careless, and it seems this fellow was pondering a new poem when he fell from Dubrovnik's walls in an ill-starred moment.

In another case, a former member of the Yugoslav parliament committed suicide in Oslo, where he had followed his male lover, leaving behind a wife and two children. Norwegian newspapers mentioned that the confidential documents he had brought with him from Yugoslavia and offered to the Norwegian secret service in exchange for citizenship, were not found in the flat he had rented and where he put a small-calibre bullet through his own brain.

There was also a successful German businessman, the son of a Serbian Chetnik officer, who was not satisfied with producing quality shoes for an affordable price but wanted to sell weapons to Libya, where no wise man would do business because the Yugoslav state was already the exclusive supplier of military hardware. He died in a fatal accident in a Munich airport toilet – electrocuted when he plugged his shaver into a faulty socket. As a result, twenty workers at the airport were laid off.

And so on: The same story in every city on Olga's photos.

30

The only place where Olga supposedly had her photograph taken more than once was in the Queen Mary's Rose Garden in Regent's Park, London.

The faked photos showed Olga Pavlović standing next to a rose bush named Ingrid Bergman. I easily found that place; at the very entrance to the rose garden, where the first rose bush bears the actress's name. I stood in front of the little sign and wondered what this could possibly mean. The thought flashed through my mind that my mother's fate might have been in some way similar to that of the figure Bergman plays in Hitchcock's *Notorious*, but I had no time for that theory.

The rose garden has a small lake, and two photos showed Olga feeding the ducks. I stood on the bank and looked into the turbid water, but that told me nothing. The ducks were well fed.

Disappointed with my visit to Regent's Park, into which I had strolled full of optimism and came out of knowing even less than before, I decided to go back to the Moroccan's at Red Lion Square for some tea.

Tired and thirsty from the half-hour walk, I sat down at one of the familiar green plastic tables. A young couple next to me was loudly slurping the soup with meatballs and cinnamon. They were hungry that was plain, for the daughters were constantly bringing them new dishes. I discreetly examined the pile of food on their table. He bolted down couscous, while she attacked bun after bun, licking her fingers and even managing to drag them through the tahini in her gluttony. I ordered another pot of mint tea, lit a cigarette and mused that few things are more repulsive than people who eat like voracious animals – perhaps only people who drink like a fish.

Freud's lady friend from Conway Hall crossed the square with a takeaway cup of Starbucks coffee. Then the Moroccan came up to me, smiling amiably.

"Ah, my favourite guest!" he said.

"You remember me?" I asked.

'Of course: You stayed here nearby, at the October Gallery," he confirmed. "Am I mistaken? 'A comfortably appointed apartment the size of a matchbox', you said when you dropped in for coffee in the morning. You told me where you stayed the night and I asked what the accommodation was like. I was curious because I've had guests who have enquired about the place. Many of my guests ask me to tell them about Cromwell. But you're different to all the others – you were so completely fascinated by the story about the publican who hid Cromwell's body from the soldiers on the square! How could I forget? You wrote down what I told you in a blue notebook with a golden emblem just like the one poking out of your rucksack. That's how I remembered you, it's not every day that a man listens to the story about the hidden grave as if it was the greatest secret in the universe," I said these very words to myself a second before he spoke them.

Then, as I knew he would, he asked "*More tea?*" as he shook my hand and apologized for having to leave me.

31

Mandušić sacked me. His secretary called and conveyed the threat in a sugar-sweet voice: "The boss asks that you not try to contact him any more. He advises you not to talk to anyone about the details of your business relationship, and certainly not to write about it. The boss has been kind and approved a type of severance pay; you'll receive your pay as usual for one year more."

And so Mandušić vanished from my life, along with all those marvellous bottles of single malt he sent me while he believed I could be of use to him. The whisky was one thing, but otherwise I had no objections to his decision. Mandušić had already proved to be remarkably patient. I hadn't responded to calls from his office for weeks, and it had been months since I sent him a speech.

However, my dismissal meant that I lost my access to police information, without which the chances of discovering my mother's identity clearly became negligible. But I was not to be discouraged. I would have to think faster, differently and better.

Ultimately I still had help. Wovenhand hadn't forgotten me. His two emails – one in which he sent me details of the interrogation of David Richard Berkowitz, and the other a memo of Inspector Spahić about a conversation with one of the Višegrad killers – helped me fill in the gaps in the picture of my mother. But it wasn't particularly clear, and certainly no brighter. It felt like a bottomless pit gaping in front of me, and it was too threatening and too far beyond anything I had ever dared to imagine, even in my darkest fantasies, for me to look into it without fearing the worst. And that's why I knew I would continue to stare at that horrible mass that trickled from what was my mother; darker than the universe, heavier than lead and stickier than tar. And I continued to handle it, squeeze it and bombard it with questions. I would stare at it for as long and as persistently as I had to until I saw the bottom. That could destroy me, of course, and that made it all the more attractive. What other, pressing work did I have anyway? My investigation had brought passion to my life – be it for knowledge, truth, or something much more trivial – and I had become addicted.

32

David Richard Berkowitz was a serial killer who performed under the artistic name 'The Son of Sam'. I was familiar with his murderous opus but had never been particularly interested: I didn't care for the New York of the seventies, where he committed his murders, nor the way in which he killed. After studying truly inventive serial killers, why would I take an interest in one who shot his victims with a revolver? Still, I ended up writing an article or two about his life and work.

What made Berkowitz special is what I didn't know about him and was revealed to me by Wovenhand's email. In a letter from prison, he claimed: 'There are more Sons out there – God help the world.' His prison correspondence contains descriptions of occult crimes committed by the 'Four-P Movement', a cult based in California. He claimed to have been part of its New York affiliate.

The two sons of his neighbour Sam Carr were also allegedly members of the cult, whose rituals involved shooting at innocent strangers and torturing dogs by flaying them alive.

The cult was based in New York's Untermyer Park. Bodies of skinned dogs were indeed discovered there on several occasions. Michael Newton's *Encyclopedia of Serial Killers*, which Wovenhand cited from abundantly in his emails, states:

Reporter Maury Terry, after six years on the case, believes there were at least five different gunners in the "Son of Sam" attacks, including Berkowitz, John Carr, and several suspects—one a woman—who have yet to be indicted. Terry also notes that six of the seven shootings fell in close proximity to recognized satanic holidays, the March 8th Voskerichian attack emerging as the sole exception to the pattern. In the journalist's opinion, Berkowitz was chosen as a scapegoat by the other members of his cult, who then set out to "decorate" his flat with weird graffiti, whipping up a bogus "arson ledger"—which includes peculiar out-of-date entries—to support a plea of innocent by reason of insanity.

In October 1979, Berkowitz wrote:

I really don't know how to begin this letter, but at one time I was a member of an occult group. Being sworn to secrecy or face death I cannot reveal the name of the group, nor do I wish to. This group followed a mixture of satanic practices, including the teachings of Aleister Crowley and Eliphas Levi. It was (and still is) totally blood-orientated and I am certain you know just what I mean. The Coven's doctrines are a blend of ancient Druidism, teachings of the secret order of the Golden Dawn, Black Magic, and a host of other unlawful and obnoxious practices.

As I said, I have no interest in revealing the Coven, especially because I have almost met sudden death on several occasions (once by half an inch) and several others have already perished under mysterious circumstances. These people will stop at nothing, including murder. They have no fear of man-made laws or the Ten Commandments.

Spahić's witness told a story similar to Berkowitz's confession. Spahić found him in Višegrad, where he was a highly esteemed member of the community, a kind of hero (the inspector writes that people passing him in the street greeted him with respect). He lived modestly and worked as a builder's labourer. He didn't mind talking about his crimes. After three mugs of beer at a local pub, he confided in Spahić that he knew he would *never be put on trial*.

"So you don't deny that the murders you committed were connected to certain rites?"

"No, but I can't talk about that. I really can't."

"Can you at least give me a hint of what you believe in?"

"Listen, old man, thanks for the beer, but you're sounding like an idiot. 'No' means 'no', OK?"

"Alright. But is it some kind of Church?"

"Uh-huh. It's a Church, just like an inverted cross is still a cross. But I warn you: You're treading dangerously. Do you realize what power you're up against?"

"Can you at least tell me the name of your group?"

"*At least*? You'll never find that out."

"Are there many of you?"

"Enough."

"And where?"

"Wherever history is made. Wherever there is power."

I knew what I had to do now. I sat down at the computer, and soon a new series of deaths opened up in front of me.

33

In each of the cities where I established that a member of Yugoslav émigré circles died under peculiar circumstances, an as-yet-unsolved occult murder also occurred.

A teenage boy died on Kaptol Hill in Zagreb. Street sweepers found him leaning up against the wall of the cathedral, his veins slashed. Judgement was passed: He had been listening to 'heavy metal', whose dark messages had driven him to suicide. Instead of searching for the killer, the police spent their efforts writing a communiqué about the harmfulness of the 'obscure music our young people are exposed to'.

In Brussels, in a lane behind Le Plaza Hotel, a bag of human organs and scraps of wax was found beside a rubbish skip.

In London, the bodies of a young man and a young woman were found on a houseboat moored in the canal near Camden Market. The investigation was quick to establish a heroin overdose. But what then was the explanation for the small, hidden shrine discovered on the boat, and the decapitated crows sacrificed to whatever power they (the killers or the killed?) believed in?

In Ohrid, Macedonia, the waters of the lake washed ashore the bloated, badly decomposed body of an old woman with eyes and tongue missing. Had fish eaten them because the body was in the water for so long?

Another teenage death was reported, this time from Oslo; the young man had been obsessed with the devil and listened to 'heavy metal'.

In Dubrovnik, a girl committed suicide by hanging herself from a beam in her parents' high-ceilinged drawing room. No one was worried that there was no chair at the spot where she died. How did she get up high enough? And did she shove the crucifix into her vagina herself, in a moment of derangement before death?!

In Frankfurt, at the main cemetery, someone dug up the corpse of a child that had died of a rare tropical disease that made its body rot and its brain turn to mush. The disease left the doctors dumfounded, all the more so because, as far as they knew in their ignorance, there was no kind of insect in Frankfurt capable of transmitting such a disease. No one cared about the details; for example, the flayed dog skin that had been draped about the gravestone, a little angel spreading its wings above the child.

At Munich airport, on a remote part of the runway, a pool of human blood and the mutilated bodies of three dogs were found.

In some places, the ritual crime occurred just one week after the 'natural' death of the émigré, in others it was a whole year earlier or later. But the pattern was clear. I had marked the killings of émigrés on a map of Europe with blue dots, and now I designated the ritual crimes on it in red. Even when confused, our brain strives for some form of order, and then, after establishing order where there was none, we cause even more chaos... I thought that the map, and with it the portrait of my mother, would only be complete when I was able to link the locations of all the killings and end up with a perfect circle. I took a felt-tip and began joining the locations of the crimes. It was far from being a circle. I moved back a few steps and tried to imagine what shape I would get if I traced the lines further, towards the margins of the map. And then, in my mind, I saw a number nine stretching across all of Europe.

34

I stood perplexed in front of the number, but it didn't mean anything to me. Still, it was a clear and unmistakable sign, and it was up to me to interpret it.

I sat down at the computer and set about searching for information about the number nine and its role in occult rites.

The first website I opened confronted me with a Protestant pastor: 'The number nine is important to the followers of occult teachings mainly because of their perverse enjoyment in Jesus' death, which was marked with the number nine,' he thundered.

The key to the interpretation he presented lay in the Gospel of Mark in the New Testament: "And at the ninth hour Jesus cried with a loud voice, '*Eloi, Eloi, lama sabachtani?*' – 'My God, my God, why hast thou forsaken me?' And some of the bystanders hearing it said, 'Behold, he is calling Elijah.' And one ran and, filling a sponge full of vinegar, put it on a reed and gave it to him to drink, saying, 'Wait, let us see whether Elijah will come to take him down.' And Jesus uttered a loud cry, and breathed his last."

Mark thus claims that Jesus died at the ninth hour. I asked myself when that was, by our reckoning. The answer was not easy to find. The more I looked into the issue, the less I knew – almost as little as the self-declared authorities on biblical matters. I read debates about whether Jesus was really crucified on a Friday, or if it was a Wednesday. And both sides, needless to say, were in possession of convincing arguments.

That strengthened my conviction that history is fiction, as is every confession, not to mention people's memoirs. It is just as dogmatic to interpret history from a history textbook as it is on the basis of conspiracy theories. Whether we read a printed page or search with a candle in the margins for what was written in lemon juice – we will ultimately make our own story anyway, becoming the narrator of what we believe in and hold to be the truth. Every one of our truths will be our own, and our own account. There is only one kind of storyteller; the unreliable. There is only one kind of authorship; the unreliable. Even God is unreliable as an author, so what do you expect of everyone else? In the end, poetry would seem to be the least fictional medium, since it was the very first to forsake any pretence of so-called objective truth. To learn about the First World War from Trakl, the holocaust from Celan, capitalism from Pound and communism from Brecht is the only thing that makes sense.

* * *

What caused people to doubt St. Mark's account? In Jesus' time, the Jewish day began at nightfall and lasted until the following night. The Roman day began at dawn, at six o'clock in the morning, and lasted twelve hours, until six in the afternoon. How did Mark calculate time; as a Jew or a Roman? When I Googled the text of the New Testament, it was clear from St. Mark's description that Jesus was crucified in the daylight.

I remembered Maria's email and opened it again. *The ninth hour by the Church's reckoning of time, which would soon be replaced by the mercantile way, began at what we today call two in the afternoon and lasted until three*, she wrote.

I could rely on Maria and Le Goff, and felt that we had resolved that question satisfactorily.

So much for the Christians and their ninth hour! But more than that, I was interested in what the *occultists* thought about that hour. They evidently attached great significance to numbers and even had a special name for the discipline: Gematria. Also, as I was to learn, they considered nine to be a perfect number, one that *always returns to itself*. Nine, I read, "is a snake that bites its own belly – a snake consuming itself". It is the number of the full circle. The sum of the numbers denoting a full circle, 360 degrees, 3+6+0, is nine. The sum of all the numbers up to nine, I read further, 1+2+3+4+5+6+7+8, is thirty-six. 3+6=9. When we add the number nine itself to that sum, we get 45. Even the mathematically challenged with no feel for systems of numbers can see where this is heading; naturally, 4+5 equals 9.

Moreover, if we vertically order all the numbers gained by multiplying the number nine by the numbers 1 to 10, we end up with an unusual order; the column on the left consists of the numbers 1 to 9, while the column on the right is an inversion of it, made up of the numbers from 9 to 0 in descending order.

9
18
27
36
45
54
63
72
81
90

There are people, I discovered, who believe that a person's date of birth reveals the number in whose power they will live – the number that conceals the secret of their destiny. I decided to play the game. I was born on 1.5.1983. 1+5+1+9+8+3 make 27, which means that my dominant number is 2+7, i.e. 9.

Hang on, I thought, let me check if there are any other nines in my life. Olga was born on 9.5.1930, for example. I added up the numerals of her date of birth and ended up with the number 27 once more, i.e. 2+7, again nine. When did Olga die? 5.8.2003. Add up 5+8+2+0+0+3, and what do you get? Eighteen. 1+8, damn it, equals nine.

I visited the site unhypnotize.com and found out an interesting thing. The book *Numbers: Their Occult Power and Mystic Virtues* by W. W. Wescott apparently describes the importance of the number nine for the Freemasons – "There is a Masonic order of Nine Elected knights, in which nine roses, nine lights and nine knocks are used." The number nine, it says, is the number of the Earth 'under the power of evil'.

Looking through Google's results for the search string 'number 9 and the occult' then bought me back to my date of birth. The first of May, as it turned out, was the second day of Beltane, the great pagan festival (or satanic, depending on your source). Beltane is an old celebration of fertility and the Earth goddess. The Celts sacrificed animals in the Scottish highlands on Beltane, I read, but every fifth year they also sacrificed humans, usually condemned criminals and prisoners of war.

The Beltane revellers light a bonfire of nine different kinds of wood and dance around it naked. They drive a large shaft into the ground, which clearly has a phallic function. Then they dance around it in circles, the women clockwise and the men anticlockwise. It is as if their bodies form the two hands of a clock moving away from each other, until they meet again (at the point where the watch shows the number three – the ninth hour – I wondered?).

Later I came across a Christian blog where priests offered advice to survivors of ceremonies that involved ritual abuse.

The priests claimed that ritual abuse took place at three levels: As physical, spiritual and mental torture. As examples of physical torture they cited gang rape, the breaking of bones, hanging by the legs, the severing of body parts, burying a person alive, locking them in a cage, and lowering them into holes full of insects or snakes – basically the standard repertoire of horror and porno films.

Spiritual torture involved breaking the victim's will and making them believe there was no hope. The priests claimed they had come across cases where women were forced to bear children that the cult members took away from them at birth, or they were made to choose which other victims would be killed. During this abuse, their tormentors would read out from occult texts they believed in.

The aim of mental torture, in turn, was to ensure that victims remained members of the cult, even if they led a seemingly normal life or kept returning voluntarily to rites such as the Black Mass and Beltane; and, most importantly, that they never reported their tormenters to the authorities.

With most victims, ritual abuse became their lot at a very early age. Where did those children find comfort? In what we usually all too lightly call madness, the priests claimed on their blog. Those who managed to dissociate themselves from the horror would survive. They created a dissociative identity for themselves, I read – what psychiatrists used to call multiple personality disorder. I searched for a definition of dissociative identity disorder and felt a wrenching coldness, as if I had just opened a freezer where a gruesome secret was waiting for me. *Dissociative disorders or dissociative identity disorders*, it said on the screen, *are marked by changes in a person's sense of identity, their memory or consciousness. People with this disorder can forget important events from their past, or temporarily forget who they are, or even assume a new identity. They can leave their habitual environment and wander off. In an episode of depersonalization, people quite suddenly lose the feeling of their own ego. They can feel they have left their own body and are observing themselves from the outside. Sometimes they move as if they are sleepwalking, in a world that has lost its reality. Similar, but more intensive episodes occasionally occur in schizophrenia. However, the experiences of the schizophrenic person do not have the 'quasi' quality that the person with depersonalization reports.*

This site referred to a description of the satanic nature of *Beltane* taken from Beltane (2005) by the Joy of Satan Ministries, retrieved from http://www.angelfire.com/empire/serpentis666/Beltane.html.

I couldn't check it because the page was no longer active.

I read a heated debate on www.davidicke.com/forum/showthread. php?t=168329 about whether Beltane was a Satanist or just a pagan ritual. Someone mentioned the pentagram that the Beltane fires form when seen from a bird's-eye view (or God's?). Sceptics demanded photographs as proof

So I entered 'Beltane occult images' in the search engine. The photos from a festival somewhere in Scotland showed naked people painted red. They were yelling and running across a field with flaming torches. A woman knelt in front of a man and reached out for his penis, while a couple beside them had (or at least simulated) sex standing up.

I imagined I was in a forest, lying naked on the leaves. The air was cold, but I was enveloped in writhing, warm bodies. The smell of human flesh mingled with the smell of the earth. My fingers felt damp, but I couldn't tell if it was from the bodily fluids of the woman beneath me or the moisture of the ground.

I waited for the moment when the fire of the wooden phallus in the field nearby would throw its light on us.

35

Come on, you don't believe in the devil, I said to myself. But *me* not believing, *me* knowing that the devil doesn't exist, doesn't mean *they* or *she* didn't believe. When has the non-existence of something ever been a reason not to live one's life by it and to kill in its name? Things that don't exist, but which people believe in, produce consequences much more real than things that exist and no one believes in. What is world history if not a tale of bloodshed in the name of nation and religion – those ghosts of culture and identity?

Confronted with another of my mother's terrible secrets, I did what I normally did when I wanted to forget what I was struggling to understand, or didn't dare to try: I fled from the unbearably specific into the unbearably general. Thinking about the miserable state of the world is a real consolation compared to thinking about the poverty of one's own existence. A dirty little secret common to all initiatives and movements to make the world a better place is that people work towards bettering the world so as not to have to work on themselves. Few things are as relaxing as launching into a furious tirade about the miserable state of civilization, the human race and the planet... Every critique of so-called objective reality has to end in a farce, and the proponent of a better world as a comedian. As far as I was concerned, the world was perfect: It only existed so I'd be able to complain about it. I walked in circles through the flat and recited the obvious; invoking reason in the face of their *convictions* is about as effective as invoking statistics about droughts when a flood is swallowing up whole cities and bearing down on your house and your library – your *temple of reason*.

Surrounded by people with such firm convictions and such weak reason, where can you run?

In a country where expectant parents who find out the baby will be a girl say, 'let's hope she's pretty rather than clever', and where there's no greater joy for parents than to produce a dim-witted macho to continue the family line, where can you run to?

My fury grew, and with it my hunger. I opened the fridge, but there was nothing except ice and Coca-Cola. I called a taxi with the plan of going to a good restaurant near the airport, where I would be able to have a decent meal, knock back a few drinks, and so I hoped, at least briefly forget about my mother, the shepherds, the flock and their convictions.

I got in the back. So as to forestall any form of communication, I told the taxi driver I had a splitting headache and needed quiet.

On the road out of the city we were nearly killed by a bald idiot in a BMW, who came flying into the roundabout and cut across our path.

I exploded.

"What can you do but stop that animal and put a bullet in his brain, right here by the roadside?!" I raged. 'Shouldn't the police shoot drivers like him? I mean, seriously, having a police force only makes sense if they publically execute people like that. What else is the point of a repressive apparatus? That's how it is, and that's why I've never wanted any form of power for myself. Every attempt to make the world a better place necessarily demands mass executions, and I don't have the stomach for that. I would willingly applaud, but I couldn't order killings myself. That's how things are, especially in countries like Montenegro, where the brutishness in people can only be driven underground by the harshest repression. Montenegro, Serbia, Croatia, Bosnia, Macedonia, Albania and Kosovo aren't proper states, just like Montenegrins, Serbs, Croats, Bosnians, Macedonians, Albanians and Kosovars aren't civilized peoples, but herd-like populations. You can't even regulate the traffic here without summary trials, let alone make a fairer society.'

The driver followed my tirade in stunned silence. I saw the fear in his face via the rear-view mirror. Respecting all the traffic signs, he drove me to the restaurant, snatched the money I held out to him and fled as fast as he could.

I wolfed down a giant, rare steak and ordered a double black *Johnnie*. I kept drinking until closing time, and then the waiters joined me. When we finally left the place, I was too drunk even to get in a taxi. The good people took me to a nearby motel. On the way they removed all the money from my wallet. Oh well, nobody's perfect. They were at least considerate enough to leave my credit cards. They had drunk all night on me – that's the sort of kindness that touches people's hearts – so they felt the need to return the favour.

36

Zonked out as I was, I missed four calls from Maria. When she realized she wasn't going to reach me, she sent a text message: Goran has killed himself.

It didn't fully hit me until I was in the taxi and we were driving past Lake Skadar. I needed that confrontation with the beauty of the landscape to make me register what had happened. Beauty is so difficult because it's always completely out of context and there's no place for it here. The cruelty of existence is only bearable because people are such pathetic creatures. Horrible things happen to us, and we deserve horrible things. Full stop. Whatever happens to us can be sad, but not unfair. And yet beings as pure and poorly equipped for the slaughter as Goran, ought to be exempt from the logic of existence. When what is good and innocent is exposed to the laws of the world we live in, all reason and all consolation vanish. Since that's how it is, I calmly accepted all the torment and torture, the industry of death and all the atrocities people have done to others, but fell to my knees at news of children burning dogs alive. We've been taught to live with the history of our race, which is nothing other than a history of atrocities. But sometimes the madness of so-called normality becomes unbearable. That's why I think that when Nietzsche collapsed over the flogged horse in Via Carlo Alberto in Turin on 3rd January 1889, it wasn't a moment of madness but one where his mind finally broke through all that had previously shackled it, an hour of the greatest lucidity and the purest cognition, so complete that afterwards there was no return – an hour of confrontation with horror, face to face, after which the only way of escape did lead into madness.

I called Maria. Through her weeping, she told me what had happened. Goran had taken her out to dinner the night before at the newly built hotel in the Old Town. It had been a real feast. One dish followed another, all of the very finest, accompanied by a connoisseur's choice of wines. What's the occasion, she asked him. Let that be a surprise, said Goran. She felt that he enjoyed every moment of the evening, talking about me and the three of us, reminiscing about our times together, and coming up with a host of old memories that had long since faded for Maria. They said goodbye heartily, with a hug. He stayed to finish off the bottle of Chilean red. He paid, gave the waiters an excessive tip worth as much as their Sunday pay, and asked them to bring another bottle while he smoked a cigar on the terrace: a good Primitivo, if you please. Then he went out and jumped.

37

I went by taxi to the cemetery below the Old Town. Goran's father could hardly wait to see the last of the body. He didn't want any condolences, ceremony or speeches, only for the corpse to be lowered into the earth as soon as possible. I found him at the gate of the cemetery. In spite of everything, I felt the need to say a few words and give him a firm handshake. He just stood there, visibly disturbed by the unpleasant obligations his son had foisted upon him. He didn't even look at me when I walked past to join Maria, who was standing at the open grave dressed in black and sobbing inconsolably.

Goran's father hurried the gravediggers until they had finished. At that moment, Goran's sister threw herself onto the mound. She crammed soil into her mouth, so we couldn't make out what she was trying to say, but it seemed she was begging him for forgiveness, promising she didn't know it would be like this, and swearing she had never imagined her husband was capable of doing what he did. Her father strode up, jerked her by the hair and dealt her a fierce slap in the face. He glanced at her full of contempt and then went up to Maria.

"Stop that whining," he hissed. "You should have jumped with him. You're going to do it sooner or later anyway. That weakling! As soon as he was born I knew he was weak and would bring shame on the family. I'm going now, to get away from all the disgusting things people are saying about us," he said so that all could hear him. He was the first to leave the cemetery, like an offended guest who demonstratively leaves a gathering.

Later, Maria and I had coffee at the quay, and she read out sections of articles about Goran's death. It was devastating that we as his closest friends – his true brother and sister, as he used to call us – had not noticed the glaring signs of the coming tragedy. We learned about the reasons for our best friend's death from the morning papers. I had been busy with the troubles caused by my mother, Maria had woes with her own, and we had totally forgotten about Goran, it's true. His fall lasted for months, two whole years even, and that last night it just ended on the rocks below Kalaja. If one of us had reached him a hand it may not have saved him, but at least he wouldn't have died feeling totally alone, deserted and betrayed by those closest to him.

Goran approved loans to people he shouldn't have: To poor people, when it was obvious they wouldn't be able to pay it back, and to desperate people prepared to cry and grovel in his office, to kiss his hands and bless him when he gave them the money in breach of all the bank's guidelines. He approved dozens of loans like that to people who later didn't respond to his calls, avoided him in the street, and ultimately drove him from their doorstep, hurling insults when he came to ask them to repay their debt because otherwise it would fall on him. He gave a loan to his sister's husband, twenty thousand euros, for which she had been begging for weeks; the rat gambled away a third of the money that same night and lost the rest by the end of the month in failed black-market operations. Goran also gave an astronomical amount to Radovan. That swine had money and could have paid his debt, but he still didn't. That's how people have become rich and successful from time immemorial, by abusing the trust of a good person, screwing them over, and driving them to their death.

Finally, in imminent danger of imprisonment, Goran took out a loan in order to pay off part of the other people's debts, and then another to pay off the first loan. But then it was all over. They summoned him to the bank's central office in Podgorica and gave him one week to pay back all the money, otherwise they would hand him over to the prosecutor's office and impound all his family's assets. 'This has never happened to us before,' they told him at the end of the meeting. 'Embezzlement yes, we've had that, but a case such as yours, where *you* pay off the debts of the people you gave loans to... Do you realize how much this goes against the very principles of banking?' a clerk who had been at the meeting told journalists: 'How could you believe those people?' I asked him with disbelief as he was leaving. While he was waiting for the lift he just said, 'They're good people, and in different circumstances they would have done the right thing.' She was rewarded for her confession with a little portrait at the bottom of the page – taken when she was younger and more attractive, I cynically presumed.

Maria and I sat in silence, smoking and watching as night fell. She went off to the toilet. There was excitement at the next table, one of the teenagers claimed to have seen a pod of dolphins. The others unsuccessfully tried to take snapshots of the animals with their mobiles so as then to post them on social networks. The horde of juveniles gambolled around the café with their electronic gadgets pointed out to the sea. When they finally calmed down and went back to their seats, a boy with a piping voice said that dolphins ought to be killed because they were pests. His uncle was a fisherman, and dolphins ate fish out of his nets. The girls felt sorry for the dolphins at first – they're so cute! – But in the end they all agreed that if they needed to be killed, what could they do about it? The females of the species now opted out of the debate and decided to hang around on fashion websites until the males returned from the hunt. The males, indeed, were sharing their experience of what was the most effective way of killing a dolphin? They started with the individual animal: You throw a fish from the boat, and when the dolphin comes up you harpoon him. Later they thought of mass executions; you throw a few sticks of dynamite at the pod of dolphins. Within a minute, the boys had moved on to genocide; you fill an old fifty-litre tub of house paint with nails and twenty kilos of dynamite, attach a long fuse and lower it fifty metres down on a rope; dolphins are curious creatures, and the whole pod follows the tub. When it goes off, it's like a miniature atom bomb. Nothing is left alive down there.

When Maria came back from the toilet, I grabbed her by the arm and said, "Take me away to where there are no people."

38

She insisted I stay at her place for a few days.

"We have to visit the grave. We'll do up that gloomy mound a little," she said. "His father won't notice – that swine won't be going to the cemetery again until he dies himself."

I raised no objections. That was what I had secretly been hoping. I needed Maria's company.

We ate dinner in silence. Tereza had cooked swordfish, which was just perfect and afterwards she served cake, although we didn't touch it. I couldn't take my eyes off her huge belly. She noticed, but it didn't bother her; she seemed to enjoy the attention it brought. It was only one more month until the baby was due, and Maria offered that she could move into the outhouse where her father had once lived. She could live there with the child, and her obligations at the villa would be reduced to a sensible minimum. "You're a good worker, and it's hard to find the like of you," Maria told her. Tereza gladly accepted and called Maria her patron. She was constantly giving her new crosses from Ostrog Monastery, which Maria put away in a drawer of her wardrobe.

"We haven't seen each other for such a long time," I said to Maria when she had sent Tereza off to bed. "There are so many things I've been meaning to tell you, but now I just want to sleep. My strength is giving way and my head is empty."

"And your heart?" she teased. "No, no, off you go. I'm tired myself. There's always tomorrow. Everything will be better in the morning."

39

She lied so I wouldn't feel guilty. She didn't go to bed herself. When I came down for breakfast, I found her sleeping on the sofa in the drawing room with an empty bottle of wine beside her.

Tereza was waiting for me in the kitchen with an excellent espresso and freshly made croissants. She didn't stay for long because the bell with 'Mama Elletra' on it rang. The lady was awake and needed the assistance of the servants. Tereza darted off upstairs like a whirlwind.

Wovenhand wrote again. Like his previous emails, this one too concealed a real pearl inside a shell of worthless commonplaces. That morning, he wrote to me about Ed Gein. I skimmed over his biography, which I knew down to the last detail. After the death of his dominant mother, Gein tailored his world and his house in Plainfield, Wisconsin, to match his madness. There were just two murders, meaning he didn't fit into the FBI classification, which presumes that a serial killer has slain three or more people. He dug up graves, snatched the corpses and took them to his house. There he made furniture with the body parts, as well as dresses that he wore, especially on the nights with a full moon. He peeled the skin off the faces of the dead women, covered his own body with it, and long stood gazing at *her*, at himself, in the mirror. Everything Gein ever wanted was to be a woman. One particular woman - his mother.

Together with Gein's biography, Wovenhand sent me an excerpt from an article by Aleksandar Bečanović, the Montenegrin film critic:

Paul Cronin's book Herzog on Herzog *mentions a less-known fact about Gein: Herzog filmed his depressing description of the 'American dream',* Stroszek *(1976), in Plainfield, of all places. 'What is exceptional about Plainfield,' he emphasizes, 'is that five or six mass murderers emerged there in the space of just five years. There is no clear explanation for the phenomenon. It sounds crazy, I know, but that's the way it is. There's something very bleak and evil about Plainfield, and even during the filming the police found two dead bodies just ten miles away from us.' One of Herzog's friends at the time was the director Errol Morris, a passionate researcher on everything to do with serial killers, who had even done an interview with Gein. Morris discovered that the graves the body snatcher dug up formed a perfect circle, in the centre of which was the grave of his mother. Morris wondered if Gein had also dug up his mother's grave and Herzog, always prepared for an adventure on the verge of reason, suggested that he and Morris meet soon afterwards and dig up the grave. But when the time came around, Morris got cold feet and didn't turn up. Herzog's comment: 'Later I also realized it was better that way. Sometimes it's best to just have a question, not the answer.'*

Clearly, my stay in Ulcinj was going to be shorter than I had planned. This time, the pointer I had received was unambiguous: *Go and see, find your mother's grave.* I called the travel agency and bought a ticket for a flight from Podgorica to Frankfurt the next day.

It had been blatantly obvious the whole time, and yet I hadn't realized – the key to the mystery could be mother's grave and what I would find there. Or what I didn't find. Poe was right when he wrote, in 'The Purloined Letter', the best way to conceal a thing is to make it obvious.

40

The villa suddenly seemed as confined as a prison cell or even a grave, and I was too excited to wait for Maria to wake up. Especially since the chances of her getting up before the afternoon were negligible.

I decided to go for a walk through the Ulcinj olive groves where Goran and I used to go and hide from the unbearable crowds that gathered in the town in the summertime, during the tourist season. I went down into town and then up through the suburb of Nova Mahala to the olive groves.

"People have told me – serious people, mind – that they've met spirits up here," Goran once said. One of them, whose words he had no reason to doubt, told him what he had experienced late one evening while returning from a walk to Valdanos Bay. Night had more or less fallen, and even in the gentle settings of an olive grove the night can seem threatening out among the trees. He could hear the yapping of jackals in the distance, but what worried him were the sounds that came from closer at hand. Somewhere half way from Valdanos to town, he heard voices speaking Italian. There in the clearing ahead of him a group of people dressed in the fashion of the 1930s were listening intently to two Italians who were demonstrating how best to prune olive trees, if his rudimentary grasp of the language was any guide. One of the instructors was sitting on a bulge in an olive tree and demonstrating how and where to cut it, while the other spread a net out on the ground, which the mature fruit were meant to drop onto. He fled head over heels and didn't stop until he reached the first lamp-posts, where he made sure he was safe.

I recalled the kindness and naivety of my friend, who himself seemed not to be of this world, as I walked deeper into the olive grove. I stopped next to a dry-stone-wall to light a cigarette. Turning, I happened to see an unusual tablet on the wall. A Star of David had been carved into a stone together with Latin letters that, to my mind, meant nothing.

The owner of the property, whom I hadn't noticed before, saw me taking photos on my phone. He greeted me amiably.

"Are you Olga's son?" he asked.

I nodded. There was no point denying it.

I offered him a cigarette.

He told me he had bought the property quite recently. It had once belonged to a family that moved away to Shkodër in Albania after the Montenegrins captured Ulcinj in 1878. Now he had fixed up the property, cleared the scrub and built walls. Here, behind the stone-wall I photographed, he had discovered the narrow entrance to a cave. It had been covered with a stone slab, and when he scraped the moss off he saw an inscription he couldn't read and 'the Jewish symbol', as he called it.

He realized it had to be something sacred. Although he was a Muslim, he respected what was holy to others. He therefore decided to have the sign and the letters transcribed from the slab onto the tablet I had photographed.

I asked him what the inscription meant. He didn't know, and he didn't want to risk his luck by offending whatever the inscription at the cave's entrance was dedicated to.

"It's been here for centuries. Who am I to change things now?" he said

I suspected that a poorly educated stonemason may have miscopied the inscription, so I asked him to show me the old slab.

"It broke," he told me. "It fell and crumbled to pieces when workers were moving it. But I remembered the inscription and noted it down on a piece of paper, which I later gave to the mason."

He took me to the cave's entrance – a shaft now sealed with a heavy metal plate and locked.

"Have you ever been into the cave?"

"God forbid, not for anything in world."

"Would it bother you if I did?"

He looked at me as if I had taken leave of my senses.

"I'm serious," I said to him. "Who knows what might be inside? I'm amazed you were able to curb your curiosity."

"I was never curious –," he shuddered, "just afraid."

It took some time, but finally I managed to persuade him to open the shaft for me. He gave me a torch and a length of rope he found for me on the property. Before I descended into the cave, he called one of the workers who were planting the olive trees.

"This man is a witness," he told me. "If anything should happen to you, it was your own decision to go in. I tried to talk you out of it, but you wouldn't listen. Alright?"

"Of course," I said.

What he called a cave was actually a tunnel, almost two metres high and one metre wide. At first I thought it was some kind of underground storeroom that had been dug for the tools needed for work in the olive grove. But the end of the tunnel could not be seen. I kept going deep underground, until I could no longer hear the voices calling me to come back. Soon the light from the tunnel entrance had disappeared too. A sensible person would turn back now, I thought. Where is this leading me? Whoever dug this subterranean passage did so for a good reason. Why else would they have invested so much effort? It must have taken years to dig. And above all - the stone with the inscription undoubtedly had religious significance...

I must have been going for a good hour when the torch began to flicker. Soon I'd run out of light, and there seemed to be no end to the tunnel. *What now?* I thought. In order to save the battery, I turned off the torch and went on, holding on to the wall of the tunnel with my right hand.

Soon I was sick of roaming through the dark, and yet I was completely indifferent to my own destiny. I felt that if this was to be my end, I would be entirely satisfied with it.

I sat down and leaned my back against the wall. I hunched up and hugged my knees to my chest. It was warm and cosy in the tunnel. The air smelt sweetish, like the caramelized milk Olga used to make for me as a child when I had a cold. You have your qualities, I said to myself, but bravery is not one of them. All your strength always came from indifference and the thought that you had nothing to lose. That's why you're not afraid even now, although you're in serious quandary. I felt my body flag and all the strength drain from me. The torch fell out of my hand and sleep came over me, quiet, comforting, like mist at the scene of a terrible crime.

When I woke up I was saved. Or doomed. In any case, I had a butt-end of life left to think about that.

A ray of light came from my right; it gradually spread until it blinded me and stabbed me in the brain. I screamed with pain. Tears welled up in my eyes, which soon saw that the way out was just an arm's length away.

The tunnel led to Balšić Tower, the tallest building in Kalaja. I crawled to the exit, which was hidden by an antique chest that I easily pushed aside. I found myself in the building that was raised in the fifteenth century, if I remember correctly, and today serves as a gallery.

Everything was clear now: The tunnel and the inscription at the exit were no longer a secret. On the wall of the narrow tract in Balšić Tower, for those able to read it, lay the answer to all the questions I had asked myself while wandering along the tunnel.

I would later write several articles about it, and even an essay for Channel Three of the Croatian Radio - about the Star of David that was carved into the wall of Balšić Tower by Sabbatai Zevi, the self-proclaimed Messiah, whom Olga had told me about with so much passion. Or rather, it was her favourite of all the lies she used to tell me. The lies of a woman whose love I can't deny and which was all the more precious because she was *assigned*, not born, to the role of my grand-mother. The anger I felt at having been lied to, receded over time. In the end, I felt only love and respect for her. She played her role perfectly and died on stage without a single gesture giving away the fact that she was acting.

Zevi was born in Smyrna, now Izmir, on 9th August 1626, on the anniversary of the destruction of the Temple. That was a Sabbath. He died in Ulcinj on 30th September 1676. That was Yom Kippur. He was forced to change faiths and died as an exile, but he was not forgotten, as Olga used to say. Olga herself seemed ultimately to believe the lies she had been taught by the authors of my life story, and she cherished the most tender sympathy for the false Messiah – she, the false Jew.

What else did I learn about Zevi from my former grandmother? There was the story about the grandiose promise he gave his many followers, who poured into Izmir from all over Europe, in anticipation of the great day: In 1666 he would lead his people back to Israel.

In the twenty-fifth year, Zevi announced he was the Messiah. He declared the abolition of God's Law. His followers grew more numerous by the day because people need hope in times of trouble – what time is not like that? – and now he called on them to eat the forbidden fruit. He publically wedded the Torah, only to later tear it up and trample on it.

In 1666, instead of fulfilling his prophecy, he converted to Islam under threat of death.

From then on, his name was Aziz Mehmed Efendi. The Sultan expelled him to Ulcinj, where he put ashore with several dozen devotees, and this was the foundation of the lie about my Jewish origins. (Or perhaps it was not a lie, for I had not learnt the truth of my background.) I have always been intrigued by Ulcinj's lack of a Jewish cemetery – and of any marked Jewish graves at all. But actually there is one: Zevi's. He was buried in the Old Bazaar, in the courtyard of an Albanian family home; the Manas. But can we be sure that it is really Zevi in that grave, I often asked myself, without having a proper answer.

Zevi spent the last years of his life in Kalaja, in Balšić Tower, where he set up a small shrine with the Star of David carved into the wall. That secret place of prayer is irrefutable proof that Zevi never really changed his faith. His spirit didn't leave Ulcinj. Even for a small town that didn't want to remember him, it was too great to push it away to the margins of its insignificant history.

Even today, the people of Ulcinj suspect one another of being descended from Zevi's Jews, who, like their master, only pretended to convert to Islam and secretly went on practicing their own religion. The townsfolk whisper about Russian Jews who have built houses in nearby Liman Cove, with a wonderful view of Balšić Tower. You can hear people arguing in the cafés that the Jews have settled in that part of town so as to be close to the Messiah, in whom they still believe, in spite of all that occurred. People in Ulcinj are dour and monosyllabic when asked questions about Zevi. The tourist guides and signs don't mention him, although he was the most important person ever to have lived in the town.

It was doubtlessly Zevi's followers who dug the secret tunnel from his final residence to the olive grove. Was the tunnel used by Zevi to leave the fortress without being noticed? Or used by his devotees in order to secretly visit him? Or was it not dug until after Zevi's death, for some unimaginable reason? Was my coincidental discovery in any way linked to my investigation about my mother and to the fact that Olga, and thus I, were given a rare Jewish surname?

The gallery was shut, so I jumped out through a window. A pack of dogs was standing there in front of me as if waiting for me. I picked up a stone and threw it at the big, black one that was the leader of the pack. It hit him on the back. The dog didn't growl or move but just stared at me, like the rest of his motley but disciplined army. To the left of me was a stone-wall, a good two metres high. The dogs' jaws wouldn't reach me there, I reasoned, so I ran to the wall and climbed to the top. I looked back and saw that the dogs were still motionless and looking at where I had been a few moments earlier, as if I still lingered there. I jumped down from the wall again, went through the narrow, urine-sprayed alley between two houses and made off into Ulcinj's labyrinth of steep lanes; so like a living organism, a creature constantly changing shape.

41

Maria was waiting for me in the garden. In her white summer dress, with her long black hair down, looking rested and fresh, and with her bare feet up on a chair, she looked like someone who had never known sorrow and had no way of knowing it because she had just come running out of the Garden of Eden. The illusion was broken when she spoke in a voice still heavy from the night's drinking spree and ordered Tereza to make us a carafe of mojito. That was the Maria I loved - wounded, wild and dangerous – allusions to innocence only detracted from her charm.

"Have you seen that Japan was hit by another earthquake last night?" she asked. Just a few hours after the ground had settled the social networks, already idiot-friendly, were hit by a tsunami of brain-dead comments, which boiled down to: 'Look, Mother Nature has sent us another warning. What will be in store for us if we keep refusing to respect her and go on opposing her laws?'

"But Mother Nature is no less a tyrant than God the Father. And not only that: Mother Nature doesn't give a damn about us. Christian and Muslim fundamentalists who believe that our cities will be subject to fire-and-brimstone because we tolerate homosexuals and their 'unnatural' practices, and Mother's fundamentalists, who believe we will be blotted out because we tolerate the disruption of the natural balance, are on the same ontological wavelength. Their vengeful mother who destroys us is just a Dionysian version of their Apollonian, wrathful Old-Testament patriarch," she sneered.

"To say that we ourselves are to blame for tragedies, whose dimensions are beyond our comprehension, because we offended Him or Her, the "One" who determines our destinies, is the most facile and therefore most commonly encountered answer. Any old balderdash that attributes "meaning" is obviously still more desirable than the absence of meaning. Meaning is highly overrated, to be sure. Never before has a higher price been paid for something that doesn't exist."

"What is in balance in the natural world? What harmony can those nutters see in the tyranny of Mother Nature? Wherever you look in this garden, some wild animal is preying on a thing smaller and weaker than itself. Everywhere creatures are dying in terror and agony, meeting a slow, painful death in the jaws of another that, *naturally*, sucks its blood and savours the head it crunches between its teeth. The harmony is just in our imagination when we watch that beauty from a safe distance. We only see the green and the waving treetops and are oblivious to the death and horror that actually reign there. So-called harmony is only visible to us standing outside, exempt from its laws. What we see is a garden to us, but for everything *inside* it is a battlefield, a slaughterhouse, where the universal code is to kill and be killed."

"And then there are all those botched-up creatures, whose design shows not only the absence of order, but also of reason. Take the hedgehog, for example. Its spines protect it against others, but the very same prickles cause it great pain. The hedgehog's strong point is also its tragic flaw. Did you know that the female hedgehog keeps putting off the birth of her babies in fear of the pain that their spines could cause when they leave the womb?" she asked.

42

The opportunity I had been waiting for to confide in Maria about all the disquieting and improbable but very real discoveries I had made about my mother came after dinner.

We withdrew into the drawing room. I sat on the divan, and she lay down, with her head on my lap and her right arm reaching down my legs.

"Don't I just look like the woman on Lucian Freud's painting *Standing by the Rags*... Don't I just!" she repeated. The thought obviously amused her. Then, with the greatest attentiveness, she listened to what I had to tell her...

"That's the way it all is, I believe," I said at the end of my confession. She stroked my face, pulled my head down to hers and kissed me on the forehead.

"What a shame that's not all true," she said. "Because if it was – if you were her son – you would have saved me from misery. That would have been easy for you. You would have saved me, and I would finally have been able to love you; because I can only love that which can destroy me."

"That's why the bond between me and Elletra is so strong," she continued, "and that's why she can run this house and my life from her tower without giving a single order. Of all the things she's done and said that made me suffer, do you know what hurt the most? It was long ago, back when she still used to leave the house and I had just made it through my teenage years. One morning we went for a walk through the pine forest. It was early summer, when you can still get through town and feel relaxed. Among the few bathers we saw on the beaches were a young man and woman. He was reading a book, and she lay with her head on his lap, softly humming. And Elletra said, 'If only I could feel the light-heartedness of the beginning again for just one second, if only I could turn back the clock to when my illusions and hopes were stronger than all the signs of inevitable doom.'"

"That morning, I had the terrible realization that nothing of mine, not even my sorrow, is unique. We convince ourselves that our sorrow is exalted, that our pain makes us exceptional, and that when it hurts we are close to something authentic and significant. But sorrow is like the large intestine; everyone has one. Even in pain you're not alone or special. Realizing that my mother had already been in the space I considered my very own sanctuary, that she thought and suffered the same way as me, yet became the picture of misery she was that morning and still is today, and that I'm no different to her – *that* was a blow I have never recovered from," Maria said.

Then she went and sat at the piano. I don't know what it was she played, but it was slow and repetitive. I stared at her long, white fingers caressing the keys made from parts of a dead elephant and soon fell asleep, imagining my mother, with her eyes closed and a look of enjoyment on her face, kneeling over a victim and gently running her finger over his dead, clenched teeth.

43

The boat seesawed on the water like a cradle while outside loud music and the hubbub of the crowd jostling at Camden Market could be heard. Drunken boys sang fans' songs, and a cheerful Pakistani called out the specialties at his stall.

I stepped over the police 'do-not-cross' tape around the scene of the crime. Below deck there was a large red stain on a white rug and two chalk outlines next to it where the bodies were found. I could see a hole made by a knife in the wooden wall of the cabin. I was interested in the shelf with the DVDs and looked for a silver case with 'X' written on it in blue felt-tip, a Verbatim disc. It wasn't there. As I was heading to the kitchenette, I passed a cracked mirror in the corridor. Despite the dark, I saw a woman in the mirror: a pale face framed by golden hair, beautiful and terrible at the same time because the eyes were missing in her otherwise perfect, well-proportioned features.

When I opened my eyes, water was dripping from the ceiling. An unbearable clamour came from upstairs. It was Tereza's voice, and through her crying I could hear her shout: *Call the police! Call the police!* I propped myself up on the ottoman and realized it was like a boat in water: Maria's drawing room was flooded. I got up and made for the stairs but stopped beside the big window that looked out into the garden. Water from the house was gushing out through it, turning the manicured lawn into a mire. Day was breaking. The first rays of sunlight were piercing the treetops. Tereza screamed again and I started running up the stairs.

Water was pouring in a torrent down the broad, winding stairs. The bathroom door stood wide open and I could see Tereza kneeling beside the huge old cast-iron bath, holding Maria's lifeless body. As I rushed in to help, I trod on something and slipped. I reached into the water with my left hand. It came out holding an empty jar of *Zolpidem* sleeping tablets. Only then did I notice that my *Patek Philippe* watch, Maria's present for my eighteenth birthday, was broken and had stopped at the number three. When I saw Maria's naked body, as white as a sheet, I closed my eyes in shame and took a few steps back; now I could only see Tereza's back, with Maria's arms dangling down it and her fingertips playing in the water.

"Call a doctor, call the police, for God's sake call someone!" Tereza sobbed.

44

Inspector Kruti held a short, routine conversation with me.

"Were you close to the deceased?"

"You know I was."

"I know, but please bear with me. It's the procedure. You're the last person to have seen her alive."

"Possibly, but I fell asleep early and now I blame myself. If I'd stayed awake I would have been able to stop her."

"I doubt it."

"What makes you say that?"

"I'm thinking of her condition, of course. She went to see Dr Milić for years. He prescribed her antidepressants, but she didn't take them."

"I would have thought that a doctor's medical ethics would prevent him from giving you her record card."

'Spare me that, please... So the last time you saw her alive was when she was playing the piano?"

"That's right."

"That's all for now. Are you planning to leave Ulcinj?"

"Yes, actually. I'm flying to Germany this afternoon. Is that a problem?"

"Why should it be? I'll leave you now to your pain. I have a long day ahead of me: I have to question all the servants and try to somehow contact Madam Elletra..."

"You're not staying for the funeral?" Tereza asked when she saw me on the stairs with my bag in hand. She didn't wait for an answer; she prodded the carpet in the corridor to check it was dry and went over the bathroom floor again with another cloth. Then she sat on the edge of the bath, stretched out her tired, swollen legs and stared at her belly. She gave a heavy sigh but was satisfied, like someone who has just cleansed the world of all its filth.

45

At least I think that's how it was.

Two days later, when I was sitting on the terrace of Hotel Catalonia Colombo in Manacor, I received an email from Inspector Kruti. He complained that I hadn't been answering his calls. The autopsy confirmed that Maria had died of an overdose of sleeping tablets. Her death was still considered a suicide, but he'd still like to have a word with me about one detail and kindly asked me to come to the Ulcinj police station to answer a few questions as soon as possible; he didn't like to think he might have to subpoena me. The tablets Maria took, *Zolpidem*, were not sold in Montenegro; he had checked my bank account and established that I had recently bought a pack of those same tablets with my Visa card at a pharmacy in Oxford Street. He was sure we would soon be able to clear up this strange coincidence.

What should I tell the good inspector? That the big picture we try to piece together is never complete? That there always remains some detail that doesn't fit into the mosaic, some trifling little thing that overturns the system we thought we had seen, something that deletes all the answers we've arrived at and opens up a host of new questions?

Should I tell him about my investigation and the blank at the heart of it, marked with a question mark? Should I let him know that that there is no grave of an Ida Hafner at the cemetery in Kronberg near Frankfurt? Should I share with him what Wovenhand had written the day before, which led me to Mallorca? Should I tell him that I already know this won't be the end, and that after my visit to the cemetery here everything will just keep on going, till kingdom come?

With these thoughts in my mind, I came across a curious news item in the copy of *The New York Times* that the friendly waiter brought me with my coffee:

Associated Press, London – The future will stop completely, claim Spanish scientists, who have devised a theory to explain why the universe appears to be expanding and accelerating continuously. Ultimately, they say, time will stop completely.

Observations of supernovae, or exploding stars, found the movement of light indicated they were moving faster than those nearer to the centre of the universe. But the scientists claimed the accepted theory of an opposite force to gravity, known as dark energy, was wrong, and said the reality was that the growth of the universe was slowing.

Professors Jose Senovilla, Marc Mars and Raul Vera said the deceleration of time was so gradual it was imperceptible to humans. They claimed dark energy does not exist and that time was winding down to the point when it would finally grind to a halt long after the planet ceased to exist.

The slowing down of time will eventually mean everything will appear to take place faster and faster until it eventually disappears.

There was a final sentence, too, where the language of science, having reached an impasse, returned to the language of poetry. I lingered over it for a long time. Professor Senovilla made the statement in the *New Scientist* magazine, describing what would happen when time finally stood still, and I recited this sentence to myself like a prayer for the comforting outcome I want to believe in:

"Then everything will be frozen, like a snapshot of one instant, forever."

THE AUTHOR

ANDREJ NIKOLAIDIS was born in 1974 to a mixed Montenegrin-Greek family and raised in Sarajevo, Bosnia. In 1992, following the break-out of ethnic strife in the country that soon erupted into an all-out war, Nikolaidis' family moved to Ulcinj, his father's hometown in Montenegro, where he still lives. An ardent supporter of Montene-grin independence, anti-war activist and promoter of human rights, especially minority rights, Nikolaidis initially became known for his political views and public feuds, appearing on local television and in newspapers with his razor-sharp political commentaries. He now works as a free-lance journalist and has recently written a number of articles for *The Guardian*. He has two other novels published with Istros Books: *The Coming* (2012) and *The Son* (2013), and in total his work has been translated into 12 European languages.

THE TRANSLATOR

WILL FIRTH was born in 1965 in Newcastle, Australia. He studied German and Slavic languages in Canberra, Zagreb and Moscow. Since 1991 he has been living in Berlin, Germany, where he works as a free-lance translator of literature and the humanities. He translates from Russian, Macedonian, and all variants of Serbo-Croat. His website is www.willfirth.de.

In 2015, Firth was shortlisted for the prestigious Oxford-Weidenfeld Prize for his translation from the Serbian of *The Great War* by Alek-sandar Gatalica.